MR PUNCH THE CUCKOLD

Punch as braggart soldier (Germany 17th-18th Century)

HISPANIC CLASSICS

Ramón María del Valle-Inclán

The Grotesque Farce of
MR PUNCH THE CUCKOLD

Esperpento de Los Cuernos de Don Friolera

Translated from a new version of the Spanish text
compiled and collated
by
Dominic Keown and Robin Warner

from the following editions:

Opera Omnia: Madrid, 1925
Rivadeynera: Madrid, 1944
Espasa-Calpe: Madrid, 1964
Aguilar (3rd edition): Madrid, 1965

ARIS & PHILLIPS LTD – WARMINSTER –
ENGLAND

British Library Cataloguing-in-Publication Data
A catalogue record for this book is available from the British Library.

ISSN (Hispanic Classics) 0953 797 X

ISBNs 0 85668 541 0 **cloth**
0 85668 542 9 **limp**

The publishers wish to acknowledge with thanks the financial assistance of the Dirección General del Libro y Bibliotecas of the Ministerio de Cultura de España with the translation.

Printed and published in England by Aris & Phillips Ltd., Teddington House, Warminster, Wiltshire BA12 8PQ

Contents

Bibliography

This bibliography is necessarily selective. Further information is to be found in Cardona, R. and Zahareas, A., *Visión del esperpento. Teoría y práctica en los esperpentos de Valle-Inclán*, 2a edición corregida y ampliada (Madrid: Castalia, 1982) pp. 229-31, and Lyon, J., *The Theatre of Valle-Inclán* (Cambridge: Cambridge University Press, 1983) pp. 221-26.

1. VALLE-INCLAN'S WORKS

Obras Completas, 2 vols. (Madrid: Rivadeneyra, 1944)

Luces de Bohemia /Bohemian Lights, trans. A. Zaraheas and G. Gillespie (Edinburgh: Edinburgh University Press, 1976)

Divinas palabras/Divine Words, trans. T. Faulkner (London:Heineman, 1977)

Martes de Carnaval. Esperpentos. Edición crítica de Ricardo Senabre. (Madrid: Espasa Calpe, 1990.)

2. SELECTED WORKS OF CRITICISM

Aznar Soler, M., *Martes de Carnaval* (Barcelona: Laia, 1982)

Bermejo Marcos, M., *Valle-Inclán: introducción a su obra* (Salamanca: Anaya, 1971)

Buero Vallejo, A., 'De rodillas, en pie, en el aire', *Revista de Occidente*, 44-45 (1966), 132-45

Cardona, R. and Zahareas, A., *Visión del esperpento. Teoría y práctica en los esperpentos de Valle-Inclán*, 2a edición corregida y ampliada (Madrid: Castalia, 1982)

Cardona, R., Greenfield, S. and Zahareas, A., eds., *Ramón del Valle-Inclán. An Appraisal of his Life and Works* (New York: Las Americas, 1968)

Domenech, R., ed., *Ramón del Valle-Inclán* (Madrid: Taurus, 1988)

Dougherty, Dru, *Un Valle-Inclán olvidado* (Madrid: Fundamentos, 1983)

Dougherty, Dru, and Lima, R., *Dos ensayos sobre el teatro español de los años veinte* (Murcia: Universidad de Murcia, 1984)

Greenfield, S., *Valle-Inclán: anatomía de un teatro problemático* (Madrid: Fundamentos, 1972)

Hormigón, J., *Valle-Inclán: la cultura, la política, el realismo y el pueblo* (Madrid: Alberto Corazón Editor,1972)

Hormigón, J., *Valle-Inclán: cronología, escritos dispersos, epistolario* (Madrid: Fundación Banco Exterior, 1987)

Lima, R., *Valle-Inclán: The Theatre of his Life* (Columbia: University of Missouri Press, 1988)

Lyon, J., *The Theatre of Valle-Inclán* (Cambridge: Cambridge University Press, 1983)

Risco, A., *El demiurgo y su mundo: hacia un nuevo enfoque de la obra de Valle-Inclán* (Madrid: Gredos, 1977)

Rubia Barcia, J., *Mascarón de proa: aportaciones al estudio de la vida y obra de Valle-Inclán* (La Coruña: Edicios do Castro, 1983)

Smith, V, *Ramón del Valle-Inclán* (New York: Twayne, 1973)

Zahareas, A., 'Introduction', in R. del Valle-Inclán, *Luces de Bohemia / Bohemian Lights, pp. 1-81*

Zamora Vicente, A., *La realidad esperpéntica* (Madrid: Gredos,1974)

3. GENERAL

Díaz-Plaja, F., *La España política del siglo veinte en fotografías y documentos*, vol. 2: *De la Dictadura a la Guerra Civil* (Barcelona: Plaza y Janés, 1975)

Ruiz Ramón, F., *Historia del teatro español*, vol. 2: *Siglo XX* (Madrid: Alianza, 1971)

Translators' note

The task of translating a deeply imaginative and linguistically complex piece of theatre such as *Los cuernos de Don Friolera* posed some challenging problems. That a purely literal version would be unsatisfactory became clear as soon as the title itself was considered: to render it as, say, 'Don Friolera's Horns' would be literally accurate but semantically inadequate. Such a title would mean little or nothing to the contemporary English reader, whereas the Castilian original is loaded with significance. It is still current usage in Spain to allude to marital infidelity in terms of 'putting the horns on someone', 'crowning them' or turning them into a '(horned) goat'. Such terms of accusation and insult, however, disappeared from everyday English early in the last century. Nowadays even the word 'cuckold' is virtually obsolete.

Indeed, the archaism of such terms in Britain supports Valle's basic contention that linguistically and socially embedded attitudes to adultery in Spain in the 1920s were an indication of relative backwardness. In his view, the Castilian honour code, with all its antiquated barbarity, should be consigned to history, as has happened in English language and culture.

The existence of distinct social attitudes to adultery in modern Spain and Britain has complicated the task of translating the play as a whole. In Castilian the epithets relating to cuckoldry (*cornudo, cabrón,* etc.) retain a two-pronged connotation of accusation and abuse, and it is this "amphibious" quality (as Lieutenant Rovirosa would call it) which, except in the case of the term "bastard", has long since been lost in English. It often proved impossible to translate such ambiguity; accordingly, we have rendered the literal meaning of such terms when facts and beliefs to do with the characters' sexual behaviour are foregrounded, and favoured a more colloquially vivid translation when the emphasis is on defamation and abuse. Thus, on occasion, the tone of the English version might appear to be stronger than, or at least different from, the original. It has not been our intention, nevertheless, to indulge in coarseness for its own sake, but rather to convey the overall tenor and flavour of the Spanish original.

Similar problems were encountered with the protagonist's heteronym, which, in Castilian, is highly suggestive. The noun *friolera* means a trifle, a bit of nonsense or frivolity; the adjective *friolero* is applied to a person susceptible to the cold. Our solution was suggested by the style of the play itself. One of the dramatic techniques Valle employs is the systematic presentation of characters as puppets. The richness and variety of the Spanish puppet tradition can comfortably accommodate a figure named Don Friolera. Although the English genre is comparatively poor, it seemed appropriate to look here for an equivalent laughing-stock and figure of fun.

The obvious candidate is Mr Punch. Although not a direct counterpart (he is also known in Spain as Polichinela), he is relatively homologous. The butt of many jokes and pranks, he is rarely allowed any peace and quiet. Like Don Friolera, he is constantly bothered by his wife, pestered by a little pet dog and ends up by killing the baby. Moreover, his speech and dealings with others become progressively more deranged. A further consequence of our choice of this conventional figure is evident in the use, in the translation, of Mr Punch's better-known catch-phrases, as well as certain names associated with his story, such as the occasional reference to his consort as Judy (a Liverpudlian translation, in any case, of *bolichera*) and to the dog as Toby. In other instances where names have been anglicised - as with the smugglers - we have attempted to convey the implications of the originals. In the particular case of Don Estrafalario it proved impossible to find a satisfactory English equivalent. The Spanish term means slovenly, eccentric, extravagant, etc., but no English synonym succeeds in conveying the endearingly magisterial qualities of the figure himself and his title, Don. The outlandish name Straphalarius, therefore, represents an attempt to give some notion of the absurd, unkempt yet scholarly philosopher embodied in the character and expressed to some extent in his name.

Our approach to the rich linguistic dimension of the play is worth some comment. Valle's later plays show a particularly sensitive awareness of the relationship between language and situation. Indeed, many scenes in *Los cuernos de Don Friolera* seem to develop not through action but dialogue. Register frequently functions as a determinant of, rather than merely a pointer to, characters' motivation and attitude toward each other. The romantic hyperbole of Loretta and Pachequín, the latter's flashy patter, the argot of the smugglers and their illicit dealings and the pomposity of the military provide clear examples of this tendency. Sudden incongruities and switches in register are, in turn, employed for purposes of self-parody and the debunking of social and cultural conventions. We would hope that these often intricate modulations, so important for an understanding of the play, have not been altogether lost in our version.

The idiom of the original runs to jargonese, contemporary slang and language of a regional flavour which would be unfamiliar to many members of a modern Castilian-speaking audience. Our translation has recourse to similar ideolectal and dialectal features of English. It is undeniable that a number of anachronisms have resulted from our decision to reflect present-day English usage in the translation of a play written over fifty years ago. However, the play itself depends for many of its effects on a clash and interplay between contemporary inventiveness and antiquated, artificial forms of speech, and our aim has been to suggest the tenor of the original.

As a general rule, we have avoided the use of footnotes to comment on difficulties of translation, reserving them instead for the provision of information which would help the average reader to understand the contemporary and historical allusions in which the text abounds.

The present version has been compiled from the editions listed on the title page. The overall intention has been to provide the reader with a reliable yet manageable text. As a general rule, the text of the Rivadeynera editions has been preferred, except where a more satisfactory reading is afforded by other versions. Punctuation has beeen regularised. For extensive editorial references and textual variants, the reader should consult Ricardo Senabre's excellent critical edition of *Martes de Carnaval* (Madrid: Espasa Calpe, 1990), which appeared too recently to be taken into account in our preparation of the text of *Los cuernos de Don Friolera*.

Robin Warner, University of Sheffield
Dominic Keown, University of Liverpool   July 1991

Acknowledgment

The translators are grateful to David George and, in particular, to Jim Higgins who literally - if not otherwise - had the last word.

Caricature of Valle by Ernesto García Cobral

Introduction

Los cuernos de Don Friolera[1] is the theatrical *tour de force* of a writer widely regarded as the most important Spanish dramatist of modern times.[2] The theatre of Ramón del Valle-Inclán (1866-1936) has not always enjoyed such esteem. In his own era the quality of Valle's dramatic output tended to be appreciated only by a small number of *cognoscenti*, and he was more widely known as a writer of prose-fiction. He was even more notorious for his cultivation of a somewhat bizarre public image and for his barbed witticisms, of which the cultural and political establishment was a frequent target. Valle's concept of dramatic art, moreover, was beyond both the technical resources and the imaginative sympathies of the Spanish theatre of his day, with whose backward tastes and methods he scornfully refused to compromise. Indeed, it is only during the last twenty years that the effectiveness of his plays in terms of stage productions rather than written texts has been fully vindicated. *Los cuernos*, for instance, had to wait until 1976 for its first full-scale production (although the Prologue and the Epilogue had been performed by an experimental group in 1926 and a projected staging of the complete play in 1936 was cancelled only because of the author's death). Hand-in-hand with such practical rehabilitation has grown the realisation that Valle is virtually the only Spanish dramatist of his time whose innovatory approach can pertinently be compared with mainstream developments in the European theatre at large.[3]

Los cuernos, the successive published versions of which appeared in 1921, 1925 and 1930, is one of the most intricately structured examples of Valle's later dramatic mode, a type of play he generally labelled *esperpento* or grotesquerie. Such works make systematic use of farcical and grotesque effects for purposes ranging from humour, irony or shock on an immediate level, to social criticism and existential or aesthetic speculation at a deeper one. *Los cuernos*, itself can certainly be appreciated simply for its exuberant comic invention (although the humour has its dark side) as a mocking treatment of the hallowed Spanish topic of slighted honour and revenge. The central action is, in essence, straightforward.

---

[1] Hereafter *Los cuernos*.

[2] See, for example, the opening assessment of Valle's theatre offered by Francisco Ruiz Ramón (p. 99): *'Desde* La Celestina *y el teatro del Siglo de Oro no había vuelto a darse en España una creación teatral de tan poderosa fuerza ni de tan sustantiva novedad en forma y significado como la dramaturgia de Valle-Inclán'* (Not since the *Celestina* and the dramas of the Golden Age had Spain witnessed a theatrical achievement of such stunning force or such profound originality in form and meaning as the theatre of Valle-Inclán).

[3] John Lyon, who, in *The Theatre of Valle-Inclán*, leans to a more balanced view of Valle's drama than many Spanish critics, considers that the comparisons of his approach with the Absurdist theatre of the fifties or with the Brechtian epic manner 'have been made simply to give Valle some kind of European seal of approval. Almost always they have been made with too few qualifications' (p. 189). Parallels with the German Expressionist Theatre of Valle's own era are, nevertheless, highly suggestive.

A middle-aged officer serving in the Customs Corps of a small coastal town is informed that he is the object of gossip and ridicule because his wife has a lover. Against his better inclinations he is goaded into the traditional role of murderous avenger of his own and his regiment's lost honour. He finally succumbs to grief and remorse on realising that he has made a disastrous blunder, having shot his little daughter rather than his wife. This ironically Othello-like tale is framed by a Prologue and an Epilogue in which a pair of itinerant intellectuals witness and comment on brief low-culture versions of the same basic story of cuckoldry and revenge.

But even so bare a synopsis hints at the important element of theatrical parody and self-reference embodied in the play. The audience is consistently made aware that the action follows lines laid down in a theatrical tradition and the characters frequently adopt or are forced into self-consciously melodramatic performances. Such a dimension alerts us to the presence of complex resonances. Questions are raised about the nature of fictional representation, about the beliefs and assumptions which govern the outlook of writers, the behaviour of actors and the reaction of audiences. The broader social culture within which such attitudes and practices are set is equally subjected to a process of investigation and criticism. In attempting to ascertain the scope of such questioning (and bearing in mind that Valle's theatre as a whole is by no means geared to abstract moral or ideological themes) it may be helpful to begin by outlining the play's relevance to the social and political issues of its era.

Although there are a good number of allusions to topics and events of the day, the historical focus of *Los cuernos,* as with many of Valle's works in the 1920s, is a long-range one. The perspective embraces the whole trend of Spanish history from before the turn of the century, a period which, in its turn, is framed by the salient myths and commonplaces of the nation's long-term evolution. To take an example: the topics which persistently distract the attention of the allegedly honour-obsessed officers in scene eight do not stop at matters of current interest, such as conditions of promotion and pension, the situation in Spanish Morocco and the influence of Alfonso XIII in military circles; their attention also wanders, with equal opportunity for displays of crass ignorance, to reminiscences of service in the Philippines (a colony lost in 1898), to assertions about Napoleon's involvement in Spain, and even to notions of racial characteristics stemming from the Roman and Arab occupations of the Peninsula. A similar process of historical conflation is evident in the play's allusions to the honour tradition in the Spanish theatre. Seventeenth-century, Calderonian motifs concerning punishment of adultery and preservation of reputation as social obligations are overlaid by clichés deriving from later, Romantic celebrations of illicit or jealous passion.[4] Moreover, the melodramas which provide compulsive role-models for the central characters of *Los cuernos,* are of late nineteenth-century vintage rather than more up-to-date stage successes. Both in the context of comparatively recent history and on a long-term scale, it would seem that

4   Pedro Calderón de la Barca (1600-1681) was one of the major playwrights of the Spanish Golden Age. Though his theatre dealt with a wide range of topics, from theology to philosophy, it is the cold-blooded, violent revenge of his calculatingly macabre honour tragedies that Valle censures in *Los cuernos.*

Valle chooses to present (at least where the outlook of his characters is concerned) an essentially unchanging set of attitudes and institutions, of which strictly contemporary issues are simply the latest manifestation. There is little need to emphasise that such a picture of a society trapped in its myths and traditions, congratulating itself on its own backwardness or bemoaning its perennial problems with equal complacency, is a hightly critical one.

Valle's vision of an underlying continuity in Spain between the situation in the nineteen twenties and the major features of social and political life during the previous forty or fifty years was by no means fanciful. There was considerable point, for instance, in drawing attention to the reality behind the rhetoric of the military dictatorship headed by General Primo de Rivera (1923-1930). It was clear to many dissidents such as Valle that the régime, far from bringing about a new polarisation of Spanish political life, was merely a perpetuation, by means of last resort, of the same privileged groups and the same underlying social order that had prevailed since 1874. The political system introduced in that year with the restoration of the Bourbon dynasty at the head of a cynically manipulated Constitution had been shaken by the traumatic loss of Spain's last overseas colonies in 1898 and increasingly destabilised by the impact of changing social and economic forces. By the end of the First World War the situation had become one of endemic crisis, a crisis which Primo de Rivera's seizure of power in September 1923 had superficially and temporarily resolved. Valle's estimation of the new régime is caustically summed up in his dismissal – allegedly in an interview with a journalist – of any suggestion that there was a genuine clash of interests between Primo and the constitutional Head of State, Alfonso XIII: 'The dictatorship was declared to save the king. The drunkard and the cretin understand each other perfectly.'[5] The entire period since the Restoration, and especially since 1898, had been marked by a rising tide of criticism, among liberal intellectuals, of the whole basis of national life, often with particular emphasis on the way Spaniards regarded themselves, their history and their cultural identity. In Valle's own case, it is true that for much of his career aesthetic concerns had taken precedence over ideological matters. But, leaving aside the disputed question of whether a fundamental switch of emphasis is involved, it is undeniable that his later works show a radical engagement with the problems and tensions associated with Spain's emergence into the twentieth century.

Valle's experiences during a visit to the war front in 1916 and his sympathetic response to revolutionary upheavals in Russia and Mexico can be adduced as possible catalysts for a heightened social awareness. On the other hand, the marked deterioration in the cohesion of Spanish society after 1917 (the year of a serious and violently suppressed General Strike and of an escalation of political pressure on the part of Army officers, as well as of a growing threat to national unity from minority communities) might equally be seen as the motive for his greater concern with politics. In the following six years class conflict intensified and governments came and went with increasing regularity as each successive crisis produced a constitutional impasse. In Catalonia, in particular, the confrontation developed into one of open warfare between anarcho-syndicalist

5   'El Directorio se hizo para salvar al monarca. El beodo y el cretino se entienden perfectamente.' See Rubia Barcia, p. 272.

workers and the forces of order in league with hired thugs. In addition, a catastrophic defeat in North Africa (Annual, 1921) served both to confirm the unpopularity and increase the touchiness of the military hierarchy, while working-class resentment of conscription redoubled. So volatile was the situation that the *coup d'état* of 1923 was not altogether unexpected, although it was bitterly resented by many sectors of society, who saw in it a return to the blatant military interventionism of the nineteenth century and regarded the régime it ushered in as illegal as well as oppressive.

Whatever the motives, the political resonances of Valle's theatre after the First World War are of a rather different order to the Carlist sympathies which had earlier been apparent. It is not so much that aesthetic and expressive concerns are less evident in these later works, but rather that such concerns by no means exclude (and, indeed, are sometimes explicitly linked to) a bitingly critical presentation of national life. In *Divinas palabras* (1920), a series of grotesque effects, ranging from the comic to the gruesome, highlights a tale of greed, lust, exploitation and deception set in a Galician peasant community; but the prevalence of ideologically competing (if quaintly expressed) modes of discourse, invariably employed to legitimise or manipulate, makes the affairs of this rural backwater pointedly relevant to issues affecting Spanish society at large. *Luces de Bohemia* (1920, 1924) takes the audience on a guided tour of the nation's capital city, exposing cynical opportunism and dishonesty at all levels of society, against a background of violent street clashes between workers and right-wing Citizens' Action groups or the police force. The protagonist, a bohemian prophet without honour, carries his denunciation of the corrupt ruling establishment to the point of enthusiastically endorsing the anarchist campaign of violence against ruthless Catalan employers as the only hope for national regeneration. *Farsa y licencia de la Reina Castiza* (1920), in a lighter vein, is set in an epoch fifty years earlier, but its theme of political crisis instigated in royal circles is perfectly applicable to the reign of Alfonso XIII (1902-1931), whose obsessive meddling was shortly to achieve its nadir with his encouragement of the glory-seeking adventurism which led to the deaths of thousands of Spanish soldiers at Annual. In this disaster, as in the Cuban débâcle of 1898, it was enlisted men and conscripts who paid the price of jingoistic bungling in high places, a fact alluded to with some forcefulness in *Las galas del difunto* (1926). This last play, together with *Los cuernos,* (1921, 1925) and *La hija del capitán*, a work confiscated on its first publication in 1927 for its scarcely-veiled allusion to a notorious crime involving army personnel as well as to the circumstances of the Primo *coup,* formed the 1930 collection *Martes de Carnaval.* This punning title ('Shrove Tuesday', 'Joke Generals' or 'Generals Acting the Goat') neatly conveys Valle's contempt for the ruling military establishment.

It is of particular relevance, therefore, that in *Los cuernos,* the theme of honour and revenge is presented more in terms of military *esprit de corps* than of the more traditional dramatic concern with purely personal reputation. The bombast and posturing often associated with the military life-style, and doubtless exacerbated in an army notorious for its top-heavy ratio of senior officers, is compounded, during this period, by an almost paranoid sensitivity to public criticism of incompetence and failure. One of the main justifications given by Primo de Rivera for his usurpation of power was, in fact, the need to restore honour and dignity to the military establishment,[6] that is, to silence criticism (the findings of a Commision of Enquiry into the Annual débâcle were on the point of being made public). The fact that the zealous guardians of their collective honour in *Los cuernos,* are serving in a decidedly unheroic capacity as Customs Guards, better known for their amenability to the perks such service provided than for their martial virtues, emphasizes even more strongly the hypocrisy of an exaggeratedly macho code which, we are given to suspect, represents some form of unconscious compensation for an inglorious record in the field. At the same time the play weaves a consistent pattern of allusions to national life in general, to economic difficulties, to working-class militancy, to cultural and institutional backwardness; and the greed which governs the conduct of local smugglers and Customs Officers alike is set in a national context of financial chicanery at the highest levels.

Before moving on to a discussion of other aspects of the play, it is worth pointing out that the strikingly modern technique of Valle's later plays is echoed in the trend of his social criticism. Where the relevance for a Spanish audience is concerned, we should bear in mind that until fairly recently the country was in the grip of a régime which had an ideological interest in stopping the march of history. Franco's Spain, that is to say, perpetuated many of the institutions and official attitudes that Valle was attacking in the nineteen twenties, and few would fail to recognise, say, Lieutenants Rovirosa and Cardona as prototypes of the gung-ho military mentality which produced the shameful spectacle of the Spanish Parliament being taken over at gun-point in 1981. But even for a British audience who have lived through the nineteen eighties there is a curiously contemporary ring about much of the mockery in *Los cuernos,* even though the central issue of cuckoldry does not possess the same degree of comic force as it has for Spaniards. Allusions to the prevalence of financial swindles and the black economy have acquired an uncomfortable relevance for our own times, as has the depiction of a widespread and unconditional belief in the priority of profit, an attitude defended by official rhetoric extolling traditional (in our case, Victorian) moral and patriotic values. We, too, have grown accustomed to assertions that our army is a fighting élite, a notion kept in view by deployment against terrorists at home or technically inferior enemies overseas and fostered by nostalgic recollections of former empire. Nor is it difficult for us to recognise Valle's satirical depiction of national culture in the broad sense when he puts

---

6   Primo de Rivera's post-*coup* message *'Al país y al Ejército'* (to the Country and the Army), which appeared in *ABC,* 14/9/23, complains repeatedly that the good name of the armed forces was being called into question by unprincipled politicians. This remarkable document would suffice in itself to exonerate Valle of any charge of unfair exaggeration either in his comments on Primo or in his portrayal of the military mentality in the characters Rovirosa, Campero and Cardona. A brief example: *'Este movimiento es de hombres: el que no sienta la masculinidad completamente caracterizada, que espere en un rincón, sin perturbar los días buenos que para la patria preparamos. ¡Españoles! ¡Viva España!'* (This is a movement for men. If there are any amongst us who feel they cannot fully live up to our standards of manliness, let them stand in a corner and not bother us in our task of building a bright future for the fatherland. Spaniards! Long live Spain!). See Díaz-Plaja, p. 10.

before us a society whose imagination is largely engaged by sexual peccadilloes, sporting heroes, crime, the Royal Family, serialised soap-operas and other trivialising media stand-bys.

The central premise in Valle's later works – that the dynamic of Spanish society has degenerated into an enactment, by self-parodying performers, of a grotesque farce – illustrates in itself how closely social criticism is identified with aesthetic and technical concerns. We might also note that in *Los cuernos,* an important relationship is established between cultural tastes and attitudes (especially where the theatre is concerned) and the more general flaws that Valle detects in the mentality and conduct of his countrymen. His opinion of the mawkish and formula-bound commercial stage of his day is closely bound up with more broadly based critical attitudes, such as his view that the naturally robust outlook of the Spanish people had been contaminated by the values of a degenerate bourgeoisie. Thus the judgement passed in the final exchanges of *Los cuernos* on the type of popular culture represented by the street-ballad – 'It's a contagion, a vile contagion, that decent, ordinary folk catch from literature' – is linked to the view, expressed by Valle in a letter of 1922, that 'the shameful state of our theatre is a consequence of the total disaster of a people, historically'.[7] In this sense, it is important to appreciate plays such as *Los cuernos* as positive acts of artistic defiance born of a determination to create new and viable forms of expression which can play their part in the larger enterprise of restoring Spanish society to health.

Such an outlook led Valle, in his later years, to forgo any serious attempt at commercial success and to associate with fringe groups who favoured an experimental approach and were in some degree sympathetic to developments in the European theatre at large in the years following the First World War.[8] Valle's fusion of artistic innovation with refutation of bourgeois or 'official' ideology places him in the mainstream of such European trends. Although there is little evidence of any direct influence, there are, for instance, suggestive parallels (at least on a superficial level) between his later plays and the innovations in the German theatre associated with Kaiser, Toller, Piscator and the early Brecht. In both we find an abandonment of individual psychology, the use of grotesque distortion – including an exploitation of puppet-effects and gesturing – and a concern to provide actors with material for consciously theatrical performances; there is a similar tendency to accumulate episodic scenes, structured in terms of strong visual effects, rhythm and mood, and a willingness to make parodic use of low-culture styles and routines, as well as a positive view of what the theatre could gain by adopting techniques introduced by the silent cinema (although Valle was scornful of the propensity of the latter to show facial expression in

---

7   *'Seriamente,* [he has just suggested shooting the Quintero brothers] *creo que la vergüenza del teatro es una consecuencia del desastre total de un pueblo, históricamente.'* Letter to Rivas Cherif, December 1922 (see Hormigón, *Cronología,* p. 549).

8   For example, that of Cipriano Rivas Cherif, who had studied with Gordon Craig and who conjoined a desire for theatrical renovation with pronounced socialist convictions. According to Alfonso Reyes, Valle often helped Rivas Cherif with his work as director of the Theatre Section of the (Socialist) Casa del Pueblo (see Hormigón, *Cronología,* pp. 546-47).

detail, so diverting attention from the gestures, poses and compositions which were, for him, the essence of spectacle).[9] There are even intriguing coincidences, such as Valle's views on *el grito* (the shout) as the natural tone of the Spanish theatre and the *Schrei* principle in works of Toller and Stramm,[10] or, on a more detailed level, the notorious skeletal tree of Kaiser's *Von morgens bis mitternachts* and the *pelele* (scarecrow-like figure) of the fig-tree in the garden of *Los cuernos*.

Such coincidences and parallels are mentioned here as an indication of the modernity of Valle's approach rather than as an attempt to take sides in the debate as to whether it is more useful to locate it in a specifically Spanish or more broadly European context. The term *esperpento*, which he used as a generic label for much of his later work, and which has been the object of detailed analysis by Spanish critics, had been in currency for half a century or more as a description of something garishly ridiculous. Valle coined it in an epoch when it was common for dramatists to introduce their plays by some specific (and often pretentious) generic definition. The formula *tragedia grotesca* (grotesque tragedy), for instance, which might be considered applicable to a play such as *Los cuernos*, was already the intellectual property of a contemporary playwright, Carlos Arniches; it was thus associated with a type of play which, although adopting an innovative approach, stopped far short of Valle's powerfully subversive concept and practice of the grotesque.

Valle, in fact, was the first of a number of Spanish playwrights this century (such as Lorca, Buero Vallejo and Sastre) to link an urgent need for reform and innovation in the theatre with a call to rethink the concept of tragedy. In a well-known passage in the first play to carry the *esperpento* label, *Luces de Bohemia*, the protagonist asserts his belief in a systematic distortion of the classical tragic mode to the point of absurdity as the only adequate response to life in a country which is itself 'a grotesque deformation of European civilisation'.[11] The action of *Los cuernos* would easily be recognised as a subversion of the tragic vision even without its numerous allusions to the canon, such as *Othello* and Calderonian revenge tragedies, to say nothing of the tawdry but popular nineteenth-century examples of the genre. But the emphasis in *Los cuernos* is much more firmly on the axis which links audience and author via the spectacle. The fact that the central action is framed by a Prologue and Epilogue in which two intellectuals

---

9   '*Hay que luchar con el cine: esa lucha es el teatro moderno. Tanto transformación en la mecánica de candilejas como en la técnica literaria*' (It is necessary to get to grips with the cinema: that struggle is the essence of modern theatre. A transformation as much in the mechanics of lighting as in literary technique). Letter to Rivas Cherif, December 1922 (see Hormigón, *Cronología* p. 548). Valle's comments on film close-ups of actors' faces can be found in an article in *ABC*, December 1928 (see Hormigón, *Cronología*, p. 338 in which he makes clear that he admires the cinema for its potential, rather than for its current achievement, which he defines as being to '*divertir deshonestamente a las parejas amorosas*' (provide titillation for courting couples).

10 See text of interview with F. Madrid in Dougherty, p. 156, and comments on the *Schrei* principle in M. Patterson, *The Revolution in German Theatre* (London: Routledge, 1981) pp. 86-97.

11 *Obras completas*, p. 1598.

witness and comment on short, low-culture versions of the story gives the work as a whole the air of an illustrated seminar. The subject for discussion is the representation of the Spanish honour code, with all the ideological questions that such a topic poses. Accordingly, the main body of the play locates a revenge drama in the context of modern Spain, and the question of marital infidelity is examined in three interrelated areas, each representative of a particular social institution.

In scenes three and nine we are presented with Tadea Calderón, the epitome of the hypocrisy governing established mores in nineteenth- and early twentieth-century Spain. A conscious champion of her society's values ('I'm sticking up for the whole town' she proudly intones in scene nine), she is, as presumed author of the tip-off, the prime mover of the action. She is therefore responsible for, and shows herself to be in approval of, the barbaric chain of events that is set in motion. Significantly, she is named after the famous seventeenth-century dramatist whose major revenge dramas deal with an intricately devised and savagely executed retribution for suspected marital infidelity. It is also relevant that these plays, in keeping with the wider Castilian tradition, treat the subject, not as a tragedy on the level of human intimacy, but as an act of obedience to rigid social norms: a ritual and essentially passionless cleansing of a stain on one's honour by means of the shedding of blood. Doña Tadea, a sanctimonious old hag, is typical of the formulistic obsession with appearances and lack of genuine moral concern that Valle saw as endemic in the society and the Church she represents. Vindictive, repulsive and decrepit, she keeps vigil, owl-like, over the social deportment of the town. A fleeting but poignant contrast to her is provided by the waiter Barallocas who, at the end of scene seven, suggests divorce in a secular state as a far more reasonable solution to the whole question.

As a complement to the sham concern with 'decency' typical of Tadea Calderón, we are presented with a view of the military (scenes one, eight, ten and twelve) who, as a class, are instrumental to the maintainance of this social order. They fully subscribe to the demented cruelty that the honour code requires and are keen to pander to its communal expression: 'We officers have our reputation to live up to ... In all and absolute truth, a fit of insanity is exactly what's required,' lectures Lieutenant Rovirosa in scene ten as he pontificates on his fellow officer's marital problems. It is not only in questions of deportment that the hypocrisy of the Spanish military is glaringly evident. The professional ineptitude of the army (as opposed to its compensatory claims to martial prowess) is lampooned in the sabre-rattling of Mr. Punch and his fellow officers. Devoid of any heroic distinction (Cardona, a pen-pusher, has never seen action), they continually brag about the imagined glory and reputation of the Spanish army, whilst the sad truth of the matter is that they are all petty officials on the take in the Customs Corps. Their moral bankruptcy is highlighted in the meeting of the Lieutenants (though they are ostensibly assembled to pronounce on questions of honour and justice, their conversation digresses readily to opportunities for corruption and the physical delights of native girls) and in the crass sentimentality of Colonel Lamela, whose moral sense is more offended, in the final scene, by the indecency of his wife's state of dress than by the reported murder of Loretta.

The depiction of the love triangle (scenes five, six and nine) constitutes a mordant parody of contemporary melodramatic treatment of slighted honour. We have already referred to Valle's hypothesis that the social and cultural decadence of the dominant classes had contaminated and enfeebled the innate vigour of the Spanish people. In this respect, his ironic send-up of the conventional theatrical treatment of illicit liaisons implies more than a criticism in purely aesthetic terms. It is also a caustic attack on the stagnant mentality which accepts and promotes such time-worn artistic stereotypes. In a grotesque pastiche of the traditional star-crossed lovers, Valle presents us with a lame scarecrow of a barber who scampers like a deformed Romeo over garden walls and trees to his buxom, middle-aged Juliet. Their clumsy, exaggerated gestures lampoon the stylised hyperbole of Romantic courtship, an effect well illustrated by the stage direction in the eleventh scene:

Loretta heaves a sigh and raises her hand to her temples. Her gallant puts his hand round her waist and with one eye peers over the laces of her robe for an eyeful of the ample expanse of her breasts.

The satire is further accentuated by frequent shifts in register as a means of ridiculing pretentious middle-class notions of etiquette. In scene six, the would-be decorous Loretta makes misguided appeals for decency and propriety in the troubled household:

MR PUNCH: I'm absolutely flabbergasted!
LORETTA: Mind your language, Pascual! You're a rough brute of a soldier, you don't treat me with any respect!

only to give way, in her exasperation at the end of the scene, to the choicest of colloquial expressions:

MR PUNCH: Trollop!
LORETTA: Bollocks!

Cementing the link between ethics and aesthetics, these specific social criticisms are framed in the structure of the play by speculations on the moral implications of dramatic representation. In the Prologue and the Epilogue, Straphalarius ponders on the various versions of the revenge drama *vis-à-vis* the mimetic relationship between author and fictional characters.[12] In 1928, Valle himself summarised the three attitudes an author (and, by implication, an audience) might adopt towards his creations as kneeling, standing or raised aloft,

---

12 A number of commentators have seen Don Estrafalario as a spokesman for Valle himself. Interestingly, in a letter (1923) to Manuel Azaña, Valle expresses himself in very similar terms to this character to ironise his feelings on reading a special number of *La Pluma* dedicated to his work: *'Los muertos deben sentir una emoción semejante al oír los responsos que aquí, en este mundo, les cantan'* (The dead must experience a similar emotion when they hear the responses sung for them here in this world). See Hormigón, *Cronología* pp. 554-55.

that is, deferential, equal or superior to them in terms of emotional empathy.[13] The first attitude is that of the epic, the second that of Shakespeare or the modern novel, while the third, is that of a puppet show. In the particular case of *Los cuernos*, and leaving aside, for the moment, the question of the viewpoint adopted for the central action of the triptych, it is readily apparent that the blind balladeer attempts to present Mr. Punch as a larger-than-life hero, whereas Fidel the puppeteer toys with him and mocks him in a condescendingly malicious manner.

The intellectual, however, adds a further dimension to the question. He contends that the authorial perspective adopted for each fictional representation of the tale can act as a pointer to contrasting sets of values in the society from which they emanate. The comical dénouement and raunchy good humour of the puppet version are preferred by Straphalarius to the gratuitous violence typical of the standard treatments of the theme. We are given to suppose that its superiority is directly attributable to the higher status that the showman enjoys in relation to his puppets. The showman is affectively detached from the action. When he intervenes, it is merely through a impartial sense of fun, and it is this emotional aloofness which anticipates the civilised outcome of the performance, in which the habitual savage retribution dissolves into innocuous bawdy merriment. In contrast, the customary barbarity of the revenge story is ascribed by the intellectual to an undiluted sense of empathy between author and character:

> STRAPHALARIUS: Blind Fidel is superior to Iago. Iago, when he unleashes the great force of jealousy, is out for revenge, whereas our other rogue, a far more refined old soul, is only out to have a laugh at Mr Punch's expense. Shakespeare puts Othello's heart in tune with his own. He opens himself up to the jealousy felt by the Moor. Creator and creature are both made of the same human clay. This puppeteer, however, at no time considers himself anything but superior in nature to the puppets in his show.

For the intellectual, an affective distance between author and characters is essential for a reasonable solution to the action. Yet it is made abundantly clear that a satisfactory outcome is possible only when it is the creative artist who occupies the superior level. In the Epilogue, the blind balladeer subordinates his status to that of Mr Punch, who is portrayed as a larger-than-life hero. As a result, the wanton savagery of the protagonist's behaviour is not only condoned but eulogised. Needless to say, there is an implicit indictment here of the values of a society which not only tolerates such savage conduct but, more alarmingly, holds it to be exemplary:

> With an axe he's hacked off both their heads,
> they lolled about so lewd,
> he's grabbed his trophies by the hair,
> that gallant soldier blue.
> He stands before his general

---

13 This interview (*ABC*, 7/12/28) has inspired much critical speculation about the structure of *Los cuernos* since Buero Vallejo's influential article: 'De rodillas, en pie, en el aire', *Revista de Occidente*, 44-45 (1966), 132-45.

and holds them for review.
It is a capital offence,
adultery, in Spain,
and General Polavieja,
as custom doth ordain,
has on his chest a medal pinned,
as if for a campaign.

Appalling artistic expression is seen as a fitting vehicle for reprehensible morality and Straphalarius is at pains to condemn such creative and ethical turpitude. The hackneyed hyperbole of the epic and melodramatic versions of the tale derives from the barbaric yet essentially passionless excesses they describe. The callous inhumanity of Calderonian precepts is echoed by the mechanical submission of characters to a predetermined and sterile code of revenge:

STRAPHALARIUS: Spanish cruelty has all the barbarous liturgy of an *auto-da-fé*.it has the coldness of every set of rules from the Spanish Constitution to the standard school grammar.

The intellectual consistently asserts the superiority of the puppet form as an expressive formula which, given the connection between theatre and social morality, can logically be proposed as a means of reforming the regressively hypocritical attitudes prevalent in Spanish society:

STRAPHALARIUS: This treadle of dolls on an old Punch-and-Judyman's shoulders is, for me, more suggestive than the Spanish theatre and all its rhetoric... Old Fidel's puppet show is the only thing that can redeem us!

An initial reading of the central action might suggest that Valle adheres strictly to the aesthetic directives for affective aloofness laid down by the philosopher. On stage, his characters are subjected to grotesque distortion. In their speech, gestures and costume they are depersonalised and given the attributes of animals or puppets. As a consequence of this technique, a distance is created between audience and players, similar to that created by Fidel in the Prologue. The military, for example, are gross caricatures, and even the lamentable and potentially pitiable figure of Manolita is portrayed at first as nothing more than a sad rag doll.

Valle, nonetheless, does not follow Straphalarius' prescription to the letter and is far less inhibited in his fictional projection, as at no time does he attempt to eliminate empathy completely from the proceedings. There is an unmistakably pathetic quality in the basic human substance on show (particularly evident in the touching exchanges between the Astete family), which imbues the action with emotional ambivalence. What the playwright achieves, in fact, is to inspire two seemingly contradictory reactions in the audience. We are induced both to look down on the characters dispassionately, as if they were mere wooden artefacts and, at the same time, to feel a genuine sympathy for them, as if they were figures of flesh and blood. The protagonist may prance about, rant and rave like a military Mr Punch, yet he also has an endearing quality, especially evident in his dealings with his daughter:

MR PUNCH: You're the pretty little flower of my life!
MANOLITA: Oh daddy dear, I love you so much!

    In this way, despite the grotesque elements of his characterisation, Mr Punch is never entirely stripped of all human apparel, and can inspire genuine pathos on various occasions, such as his halting indecision as to how to resolve his dilemma, or his strained friendship with Pachequín. His status as an individual is further affirmed by the compassionate observations of Flash Frank and Calixta in scene seven, when they remark on the unhappy predicament of this erstwhile 'good skin'. Moreover, there are certain details of presentation which appeal to our sympathetic instincts, such as the protagonist's idiosyncratic conversations with his dog in scene ten and the family's concern about the price of a guitar string in scene nine. All in all, Valle achieves a more complex effect than the straightforward distancing that the intellectual proposes since, paradoxically, the characters can elicit responses of both indifference and empathy. It is in this area – the deliberate distorting of recognisably human traits – that the grotesque element of the play is at its most powerful. The fact that the principal characters are allowed to retain something of their basic humanity lends the play a certain tragic quality. We do not see Mr Punch merely as a comical piece of wood whose actions are dictated by a savagely archaic code, but respond to him in a deeper way. There is an ineluctable element of pathos in the process by which Pascual Astete, the fifty-year-old sissy who apologetically arrives at the bar penniless as the result of a row with his wife, is cowed by the pressures of a hypocritical society into robotic adherence to rules of conduct which require the destruction of family life and happiness.

    The characters' puppet-like gesticulations, enhanced in various scenes by the watchful presence of the *pelele* in the tree, serve as a visual correlative of their compliance with the dictates of social convention. Significantly, such clockwork gesturing only occurs when they do not act autonomously but follow a pre-established mode of behaviour (be it that of slighted military honour or adulterous passion). Their lack of personal integrity and self-determination is further emphasised by the motif of blindness. In literature and art, blindness often serves to indicate a detraction from full humanity and is frequently employed to grotesque effect. As with all important elements in this play, there is a clear indication given as to the significance of this theme in the Prologue and Epilogue, where the showman and the balladeer respectively are blind. There is, however, a significant difference between the two on the level of perception. In the first case the puppeteer can 'see' (i.e. understand) that the topic of marital infidelity should receive a fictional treatment that is satisfactory in both moral and aesthetic terms. The balladeer, on the other hand, fails to 'see beyond' the degenerate conventions and values he unimaginatively retails.

    In the central action, the concepts of vision and light are consistently subjected to ironic treatment. Loretta repeats her plea of 'Don't bedazzle me so!' to Pachequín as she claims to be blinded by the blazing force of Romantic passion (although, in reality, it is by the tawdry neon lighting of kitsch culture).

Mr Punch is likewise insensitive to the 'day-light clear' innocence of his wife. Similarly, in scene seven, Flash Frank Cadenas is surprised by Mr Punch's inability to comprehend that his brother officers are meeting to court-martial him: 'You're blindness amazes me!' In the following scene the glass eye of the self-congratulatory (and self-deluding) Lieutenant Rovirosa bounces aimlessly around the table. Finally, in the Colonel's parlour, Mr Punch is ordered to close his eyes, while, hilariously, Pancho Lamela can see no trace of metaphorical blood on the infanticide's hands.

Although the character Fidel has something of the traditional blind seer who can perceive what the sighted cannot, in the play as a whole the recurrence of this motif constitutes a broad moral commentary on the nature of human ignorance and irrationality. Blindness suggests a spiritual as well as a physical deficiency, a condition befitting a group of characters who are, for the most part, incapable of critical understanding and thus unable to reject the dehumanising prescriptions of social convention. In this symbolic sense, it is appropriate that in a country where a blind man fully appreciates the 'value' of a painting, those who display rational and critical acumen are thrown in jail for putting the evil eye on a donkey.

The notion of thresholds, another deeply rooted dimension of human psychology, is also used as a leitmotiv in the play. We are dealing, of course, with an important aspect of stage representation in general, in terms of the action's supposed location, personal space and its limits, the arrangements of entrances and exits, and so on. In *Los cuernos,* it has to do with the notion of invading other people's territory, or sticking to one's own 'patch', and is a consistent source of humour (not the least comical examples of which are provided by the antics of the mischievous little dogs). Tadea Calderón sits perched on high in her vigil over the town and its deportment, while Pachequín scampers cautiously through trees and over walls as he invades and retreats from Mr Punch's house and garden with Loretta, his prize. Calixta proclaims a clear territorial demarcation between herself and Rovirosa in scene seven. Rovirosa is likewise tentative about entering Mr Punch's domain in scene ten and the latter's final dementia is demonstrated by his transgression of the Colonel's domestic sanctum in the final scene.

One aspect of this topic, the theme of frontiers, serves to add an extra dimension to Valle's criticism of the regressive Spanish state. The play's opening draws our attention to two itinerant intellectuals from a peripheral and dissident region who are engaged in exploring the Peninsula. Not only is the setting an outpost town, close to the sea and the Portuguese border, but it should also be remembered that the Customs Service, by definition, mediates between geo-political entities. Moreover, other cultures are frequently mentioned. Within Spain, the superiority of non-Castilian literatures is strongly affirmed. Overseas, the backwardness of the Spanish connection with the Philippines and Africa is contrasted with the more advanced European societies evoked by repeated allusions to French social norms and the strains of the British National anthem from a warship.

The overall result is to create a sense of being psychologically at the limits of provinciality; a feeling of being decentred, 'on the edge'. Such an effect is given stage representation in the first and tenth scenes, where we find Mr Punch at his outpost on the fringe between the land and the sea; symbolically, that is, at a point where hard, fixed attitudes confront adaptability and tolerance. Such concepts, of course, are very relevant to the cultural and political history of modern Spain.

There has been a tendency amongst some critics to suggest that *Los cuernos* was not intended for performance. The contrived, fanciful nature of the stage directions,[14] the esoteric parlance and other obvious difficulties (Mr Punch's dog; Rovirosa's eye, etc.) have been proposed as insurmountable problems for staging and, in turn, adduced as further evidence that Valle did not seriously envisage theatrical production. Given the techniques of modern stage management, such effects would not be considered a major obstacle by an imaginative producer. But, more importantly, the author's evident dramatic craftsmanship, particularly in his use of language, indicates that the ultimate goal was clearly performance. The structure of each scene demonstrates the play's effectiveness as a piece of theatre. In those episodes which are not intentionally parodic, the action develops naturally from a given situation through dialogue, free from the constraints of narration or explication typical of less gifted playwrights and traditional methods of dramatic writing. Valle avoids the convention of flat, expository stage exchanges in which the allusions and indirect meanings of everyday conversational encounters are normally kept to a minimum. The dialogue is often idiolectic and private – as initially impenetrable as a conversation overheard in the street – and the audience must listen attentively to piece the references together and work out the underlying motives.

In scene seven, for example, Flash Frank Cadenas' shady dealings and his attempts to enlist Calixta into his wily, under-the-counter activities are rarely made explicit. The conversation develops imaginatively and allusively, with all the inventive innuendo we might expect from the underworld of a port. The pair's long-standing relationship is not directly explained but must rather be deduced from their cagey negotiating and verbal sparring, around which the first part of the scene smoothly develops. Calixta's mock coyness in the face of Flash Frank's suggestive innuendo has all the freshness of spontaneous real-life banter:

FLASH FRANK: ... there's a rather mischievous bloodhound sniffing around where it's stashed and you, Calixta, could throw him off the scent.
CALIXTA: I don't get it.
FLASH FRANK: As soon as I give you his name, you'll do more than get it.
CALIXTA: That's as maybe.

Language is additionally important in the area of motivation. A character's conscious adoption of a given register, rather than to express any inner feelings, tends to function as an external determinant of behaviour along lines which frequently run contrary to basic desires and better judgements. Mr Punch's course

---

14 The stage directions have attracted much comment and are clearly important. Allusive and impressionistic, they evoke the atmosphere required in each scene, breaking with the 'realism' of contemporary theatrical conventions and throwing into relief the rigid behavioural patterns of the protagonists.

of action, upon which the play's dénouement depends, seems largely conditioned by the brash idiom of offended military honour; and this despite his recognition of, and personal preference for, the more reasonable alternatives available:

> MR. PUNCH: I'll put in for a transfer just in case this vile slander has any basis in fact... The honour-bound officer can never forgive his adulterous wife... And a decent separation just isn't good enough! Deary, deary me! If only it were!... I am a Spanish officer and haven't got the right to philosophise like they do in France.

The courtship of Pachequín and Loretta is equally revealing in this respect. Initially, their flighty exchanges display naturalness and wit, as in scene two:

> PACHEQUIN: One of these days I'll carry you off, Loretta.
> LORETTA: I'd be a heavy burden, Pachequín.
> PACHEQUIN: I can lift a bigger weight than Samson!
> LORETTA: With your gob!

From scene five onwards, however, in a process which reaches its climax in scene eleven, they seem irresistibly compelled to conduct their amorous intrigue along lines laid down by the vocabulary of Romantic melodrama. The inevitability of a tragic end to their affair is anticipated by the stereotyped idiom they adopt:

> LORETTA: Whither do you take me, you silver-tongued rogue... You'll be the ruination of us both!
> PACHEQUIN: Do I mean so little to you now, you scarlet woman?

Indeed, one is left with the impression that their adulterous liaison owes more to a mutual decision to act out the clichés of this particular role than to any stirrings of a deep-seated or passionate nature.

In this respect, the contrast between various character types in the central action is illuminating. On one hand, Tadea Calderón and the love triangle defer to the established code of behaviour. A linguistic correlative of their acquiescence can be found in the sentimental axioms and platitudes which increasingly characterise their speech. By way of contrast, the smugglers, the saloon staff and the Colonel's wife reserve the right to think and act independently. They refuse to allow their personal integrity to be compromised or coerced. Their motivation clearly depends on an eminently reasonable calculation of what lies in their best interests. Calixta, for example, roundly rejects Flash Frank's proposition to act as his stooge and ingratiate herself with Rovirosa. The smuggler, likewise, reserves the right to dissent, even when confronted by authoritative pressure to conform:

> FLASH FRANK: Now they're even talking about doing away with customs duty and that would be the ruination of us. If all merchandise could enter the country free, gratis and for nothing, then that would be the end for smuggling. What do you do? Plant a bomb.

The way such characters refuse to be constrained by any offically imposed directive is reflected in the liveliness of their speech. With conscious irony and innuendo they make controlled use of linguistic formulas rather than be controlled by them. They are fully aware of the distinction between reality and rhetoric and are never compromised at the level of speech or gesture, thus remaining life-like and thoroughly convincing. Those characters who allow themselves to be manipulated, however, adopt a stereotyped register – an extrinsically imposed régime of verbal affectation – which matches the puppet-like movements they make when they renounce individual autonomy and embark on a predetermined course of action.

At the same time, Valle is alert to the opportunities language affords for debunking established conventions. Sudden shifts and incongruities in idiom are employed as a means of satirising social and cultural institutions. The military's obsession with notions of honour is savagely parodied in Mr Punch's cuckold monologue in scene one through a continuous modulation in register, from that of the school-yard sissy, to middle-aged failure, to corrupt customs official, to honour-bound officer, to puppet:

> MR. PUNCH: If it *is* true, I'd rather not have known. What a wimp I've always been. And where do I go from here, fifty-three years old and my life in ruins? ... Just suppose I turned a blind eye to this under-the-counter dealing and made up my mind to look the other way? ... The honour principle demands the shedding of blood. Bang! Bang! Bang! That's the way to do it!

The send-up of military pomposity is also hilariously apparent in scene eight, where the protagonist's brother officers, sitting in court martial, pontificate on the nature of justice. Their weighty pronouncements, however, are mere parrot-like repetitions of hackneyed prescriptions, whose hollowness is comically shattered by Cardona's more accurate, if down-to-earth, interjection:

> LIEUTENANT ROVIROSA: ... in questions of honour I am categorically against any lily-livered sentimentality
> LIEUTENANT CAMPERO: Hear! Hear! But, for my part, I would like to point out that justice does not exclude mercy.
> LIEUTENANT CARDONA: Make him put in for an absolute discharge. The Army has no room for bloody cuckolds.

Valle employs the same technique to lampoon the decadent convention of adulterous passion. As his courtship of Loretta staggers towards its climax, Pachequín's powers of expression are increasingly unable to sustain the required lofty idiom. Thus, in scene eleven, he plunges from the heady heights of Romantic hyperbole straight into the bathos of red-light smooth-talk:

> PACHEQUIN: Torment of my every hour!
> LORETTA: Tyrant of my soul! ...
> PACHEQUIN: Shady lady!
> LORETTA: My ruination!

PACHEQUIN: Fit tart!

Equally amusing is his lapse from stylised affectation at the end of scene five: 'Let us cut, Loretta, this Gordian knot', to the legalese jargon which accompanies his entrance in scene six: 'Aren't you satisfied by the fact that the party of the first instance has made an appearance on your premises to effect due restitution of your lawful spouse?'

Language thus becomes a key ideological feature of the play. Idiomatic incongruities and variations are employed to discredit regressive institutions (such as the Army, the Church and Melodrama). What is more, the linguistic structure of the play has its own significant dynamism. We move from the spontaneous and pluralistic diversity of dialogue in the Prologue and early scenes to monochrome and stereotyped platitudes and, eventually, to the cold austerity of monologue in the ballad, the official final version of the tale. Tragically, the codified rhetoric of the military triumphs (as had earlier the hyperbole of Romantic passion) over the initial wit and inventiveness of the protagonists. As the plot unfolds they lose the very personal ability to be imaginative and even idiosyncratic in their expression, and are progressively forced into the official strait-jacket of uniformity and anonymity. Concomitantly, their blind obedience to pre-established models of behaviour compromises their autonomy as individuals, an effect depicted visually by impairment of human mobility and subordination to the rigid, staccato gesturing of clockwork marionettes.

Valle was clearly convinced of the importance of the theatre and the possibilities of its contribution to national regeneration. Yet in his portrayal of certain figures as puppets conditioned by limitations of register, the playwright does much more than speculate on the moral implications of differing perspectives in drama. Valle, unlike Straphalarius, is not so complacent as to ascribe the current predicament of his country to pernicious notions of fictional representation. Had he subscribed to the philosophy of art proposed by the intellectual, the characters of *Los cuernos* would have been presented exclusively as dehumanised puppets. Although Valle mercilessly lampoons particular classes and institutions, his social critique is more comprehensively directed at an endemic failing in the community at large. The self-consciously melodramatic performance of the majority of characters betrays an unwillingness to reject establishment values that are thoroughly reprehensible. When placed in a problematical situation, they forgo the freedom to act in a reasonable, autonomous fashion and, though aware of available alternatives, are consistently cajoled into robotic compliance with archaic formulas. It is the wilful self-subjugation of the individual to these anachronistic norms – a surrender which constitutes in itself a tacit acceptance of them – that is the chief target of Valle's criticism.

In other words, a generalised tendency to accept and conform is held to be just as blameworthy as institutional decadence itself. It is for this reason that Valle's vision of Spain in the nineteen twenties as a grotesque distortion of modern European civilisation has a more universal validity. For all its humour and aesthetic intricacy, *Los cuernos* carries a serious warning for all of us: it is only through rejection of complacency and constant critical vigilance that an equitable and progressive society can be established and maintained.

Bululu as depicted by Goya.

Ramón María del Valle Inclán

THE GROTESQUE FARCE OF
MR PUNCH THE CUCKOLD

(Esperpento de los cuernos de don Friolera)

DRAMATIS PERSONAE

DON ESTRAFALARIO y
DON MANOLITO, intelectuales
UN BULULU
y *SUS CRISTOBILLAS.*
El teniente *DON FRIOLERA,*
DOÑA LORETA, su mujer y
MANOLITA, fruto de esta pareja
PACHEQUIN, barbero marchoso.
DOÑA TADEA, beata cotillona.

NELO EL PENEQUE,
EL NIÑO DEL MELONAR y
CURRO CADENAS, matuteros.

DOÑA CALIXTA la de los billares.

BARALLOCAS, mozo de
los billares.
Los tenientes
DON LAURO ROVIROSA,
DON GABINO CAMPERO y
DON MATEO CARDONA,
EL CORONEL y *LA CORONELA.*

UN CIEGO ROMANCISTA.
UN CARABINERO.
MERLIN, perrillo de lanas.
UNA COTORRA.

La acción en San Fernando del Cabo,
perla marina de España,

STRAPHALARIUS and
IMMANUEL, intellectuals
A SHOWMAN
and HIS PUPPETS.
Lieutenant MR PUNCH,
LORETTA, his wife, and
MANOLITA, the fruit of this union.
PACHEQUIN, a jazzy barber.
DOÑA TADEA, a sanctimonious old
    gossip.
MANNY THE JUG-HEAD,
THE CANTELOUPE KID and
FLASH FRANK CADENAS,
    smugglers.
CALIXTA, who runs the billiard
    saloon.
BARALLOCAS, waiter in the billiard
    saloon.
Lieutenants
LAURO ROVIROSA,
GABINO CAMPERO and
MATEO CARDONA,
THE COLONEL and HIS LADY
    WIFE.
A BLIND STREET-BALLADEER.
A CARABINEER.
TOBY, a small poodle.
A PARROT.

The action takes place in San
Fernando del Cabo, Spain's
Maritime Jewel.

Prólogo

Las ferias de Santiago el Verde, en la raya portuguesa. El corral de una posada, con entrar y salir de gentes, tratos, ofertas y picardeo. En el arambol del corredor, dos figuras asomadas: boinas azules, vasto entrecejo, gozo contemplativo casi infantil y casi austero, todo acude a decir que aquellas cabezas son vascongadas. Y así es lo cierto. El viejo rasurado, expresión mínima y dulce de lego franciscano, es Don Manolito el Pintor. Su compañero, un espectro de antiparras y barbas, es el clérigo hereje que ahorcó los hábitos en Oñate; la malicia ha dejado en olvido su nombre, para decirle Don Estrafalario. Corren España por conocerla, y divagan alguna vez proyectando un libro de dibujos y comentos.

DON ESTRAFALARIO: ¿Qué ha hecho usted esta mañana, Don Manolito? ¡Tiene usted la expresión del hombre que ha mantenido una conversación con los ángeles!

DON MANOLITO: ¡Qué gran descubrimiento, Don Estrafalario! ¡Un cuadro muy malo, con la emoción de Goya y del Greco!

DON ESTRAFALARIO: ¿Ese pintor no habrá pasado por la Escuela de Bellas Artes?

DON MANOLITO: No ha pasado por ninguna escuela. ¡Hace manos de seis dedos, y toda clase de diabluras con azul, albayalde y amarillo!

DON ESTRAFALARIO: ¡Debe ser un genio!

DON MANOLITO: ¡Un bárbaro! ... ¡Da espanto!

DON ESTRAFALARIO: ¿Y dónde está ese cuadro, Don Manolito?

DON MANOLITO: Lo lleva un ciego

DON ESTRAFALARIO: Ya lo he visto.

DON MANOLITO: ¿Y qué?

DON ESTRAFALARIO: Que si usted quiere, lo compraremos a medias.

DON MANOLITO: El tuno que lo lleva, no lo vende.

DON ESTRAFALARIO: ¿Se lo ha puesto usted en precio?

DON MANOLITO: ¡Naturalmente! ¡Y se lo pagaba bien! ¿Llegué a ofrecerle hasta tres duros!

DON ESTRAFALARIO: En cinco puede ser que nos lo deje.

DON MANOLITO: Vale ese dinero. ¡Hay un pecador que se ahorca, y un diablo que ríe, como no los ha soñado Goya! ... Es la obra maestra de una pintura absurda. Un Orbaneja de genio. El Diablo saca la

Prologue

The fair of Santiago el Verde, on the Portuguese border. The yard of an inn; people wandering in and out. Wheelings and dealings; the crack is fierce. Against the back curtains of a balcony two figures stand out: blue berets, eyebrows far apart, a delight in contemplation, almost child-like, almost austere. Everything points to the fact that the two figures are Basque. That is the truth of the matter. The clean-shaven oldster, with the sweet, minimal expression of a lay Franciscan, is Immanuel the Painter. His companion, a spectre in beard and spectacles, is the heretical cleric who hung up his cassock in Oñate. Malice has left his name in oblivion, so he is known merely as Straphalarius. They are travelling round Spain to get to know the country and occasionally digress as they plan a book of drawings and commentaries.

STRAPHALARIUS: What have you been up to this morning, Immanuel? You have the look of one who's just conversed with the angels!

IMMANUEL: A rare old discovery, Straphalarius! A really evil painting, with the emotional force of a Goya or an El Greco!

STRAPHALARIUS: Won't this painter have been to the School of Fine Art?

IMMANUEL: He hasn't attended any school at all. He draws hands with six fingers and gets up to all sorts of devilry with blue, ceruse and yellow!

STRAPHALARIUS: He must be a genius!

IMMANUEL: He's out of this world! ... It really takes your breath away!

STRAPHALARIUS: And where is this painting, Immanuel?

IMMANUEL: In the hands of a blind man.

STRAPHALARIUS: I've already seen it.

IMMANUEL: And what do you think?

STRAPHALARIUS: If you're in agreement, we could go halves on it

IMMANUEL: The old rogue won't part with it.

STRAPHALARIUS: Did you make him an offer?

IMMANUEL: Of course, I did! A princely sum at that! I went as high as three bob!

STRAPHALARIUS: He might let us have it for five.

IMMANUEL: It's well worth the money. There's a poor sinner hanging himself and a devil laughing, both of them beyond Goya's wildest dreams... It's a masterpiece of the absurd, with all the inspiration of an Orbaneja.[1] The Devil's got his tongue sticking out and is

---

1 An artist, mentioned twice in *Don Quixote*, so devoid of skill that whatever he depicted had to be labelled underneath in order to be recognised. Given Valle's fondness for satirical allusion, it is also worth recalling the full surname of Spain's ruling General: Primo de Rivera y Orbaneja.

lengua y guiña el ojo, es un prodigio. Se siente la carcajada. Resuena.

DON ESTRAFALARIO: También a mí me ha preocupado la carantoña del Diablo frente al Pecador. La verdad es que tenía otra idea de las risas infernales; había pensado siempre que fuesen de desprecio, de un supremo desprecio, y no. Ese pintor absurdo me ha revelado que los pobres humanos le hacemos mucha gracia al Cornudo Monarca. ¡Ese Orbaneja me ha llenado de dudas, Don Manolito!

DON MANOLITO: Esta mañana apuró usted del frasco, Don Estrafalario. Está usted algo calamocano.

DON ESTRAFALARIO: ¡Alma de Dios, para usted lo estoy siempre! ¿No comprende usted que si al Diablo le hacemos gracia los pecadores, la consecuencia es que se regocija con la Obra Divina?

DON MANOLITO: En sus defectos, Don Estrafalario.

DON ESTRAFALARIO: ¡Que cae usted en el error de Manes! La Obra Divina está exenta de defectos. No crea usted en la realidad de ese Diablo que se interesa por el sainete humano y se divierte como un tendero. Las lágrimas y la risa nacen de la contemplación de cosas parejas a nosotros mismos, y el Diablo es de naturaleza angélica. ¿Está usted conforme, Don Manolito?

DON MANOLITO: Póngamelo usted más claro, Don Estrafalario. ¡Explíquese!

DON ESTRAFALARIO: Los sentimentales que en los toros se duelen de la agonía de los caballos, son incapaces para la emoción estética de la lidia. Su sensibilidad se revela pareja de la sensibilidad equina, y por caso de cerebración inconsciente, llegan a suponer para ellos una suerte igual a la de aquellos rocines destripados. Si no supieran que guardan treinta varas de morcillas en el arca del cenar, crea usted que no se conmovían. ¿Por ventura los ha visto usted llorar cuando un barreno destripa una cantera?

DON MANOLITO: ¿Y usted supone que no se conmueven por estar más lejos sensiblemente de las rocas que de los caballos?

winking his eye. It's fantastic. You can hear the guffaw ringing
out.

STRAPHALARIUS: I, too, have been perturbed by the leer on the Devil's gob
as he contemplates the sinner. To tell you the truth, I always had
a very different idea about hellish laughter. I somehow thought it
would be full of disdain, supreme disdain, and yet that's not the
case. That absurd painting has shown me that we poor sinners
provide Auld Hornie with a good deal of entertainment. That
brush-pusher has filled me full of doubt, Immanuel!

IMMANUEL: You've had a wet of the whistle this morning, Straphalarius.
You're not fully *compos mentis*.

STRAPHALARIUS: Why, dear heart, as far as you're concerned I'm never any
other way! Don't you realise that if the Devil finds us sinners
entertaining, we can only conclude that he is highly amused by
the Divine Order?

IMMANUEL: By its defects, Straphalarius.

STRAPHALARIUS: You're making the same mistake as the Manicheans![1] The
divine order is free from defects. Don't go believing for one
moment in a Devil who is the slightest bit interested in our
human farce, rubbing his hands together at it like some
shopkeeper. Laughter and tears stem from the observation of
things that are the same as ourselves, whereas the Devil is, by
nature, angelic. Are you with me, Immanuel?

IMMANUEL: Would you care to elucidate that point, Straphalarius? Pray
explain yourself.

STRAPHALARIUS: Those sentimentalists who are distressed by the last throes
of horses at bullfights are incapable of appreciating the aesthetic
emotion of the fight. It's clear their sensitivity is on the same
level as that of the horse and by dint of an unconscious mental
process they come to fancy for themselves a fate similar to that of
the disembowelled nags. If they had no idea that they themselves
had thirty yards of black pudding in their own bread-baskets, you
can rest assured that they wouldn't feel the slightest sympathy.
Have you, by any chance, ever seen anyone shed a tear when a
drill rips the innards out of a quarry?

IMMANUEL: And it's your supposition that these people remain unmoved
because in terms of sensitivity they feel closer to horses than to
rocks?

---

1   The Manichean heresy postulates a Creation in which the principle of evil
coexists absolutely with that of good.

DON ESTRAFALARIO: Así es. Y paralelamente ocurre lo mismo con las cosas que nos regocijan. Reservamos nuestras burlas para aquello que nos es semejante.

DON MANOLITO: Hay que amar, Don Estrafalario. La risa y las lágrimas son los caminos de Dios. Ésa es mi estética y la de usted.

DON ESTRAFALARIO: La mía no. Mi estética es una superación del dolor y de la risa, como deben ser las conversaciones de los muertos, al contarse historias de los vivos.

DON MANOLITO: ¿Y por qué sospecha usted que sea así el recordar de los muertos?

DON ESTRAFALARIO: Porque ya son inmortales. Todo nuestro arte nace de saber que un día pasaremos. Ese saber iguala a los hombres mucho más que la Revolución Francesa.

DON MANOLITO: ¡Usted, Don Estrafalario, quiere ser como Dios!

DON ESTRAFALARIO: Yo quisiera ver este mundo con la perspectiva de la otra ribera. Soy como aquel mi pariente que usted conoció, y que una vez, al preguntarle el cacique,[1] qué deseaba ser, contestó: "Yo, difunto."

En el corral de la posada, y al cobijo del corredor, se ha juntado un corro de feriantes. Bajo la capa parda de un viejo ladino revelan sus bultos los muñecos de un teatro rudimentario y popular. El bululú teclea un aire de fandango en su desvencijada zanfoña, y el acólito, rapaz lleno de malicias, se le esconde bajo la capa, para mover los muñecos. Comienza la representación.

EL BULULU: ¡Mi Teniente Don Friolera, saque usted la cabeza de fuera!

VOZ DE FANTOCHE: Estoy de guardia en el cuartel.

EL BULULU: ¡Pícara guardia! La bolichera, mi Teniente Don Friolera, le asciende a usted a coronel.

VOZ DE FANTOCHE: ¡Mentira!

EL BULULU: No miente el ciego Fidel.

El fantoche, con los brazos aspados y el ros en la oreja, hace su aparición sobre un hombro del compadre, que guiña el ojo cantando al son de la zanfoña.

EL BULULU: ¡A la jota jota, y más a la jota, que Santa Lilaila parió una marmota! ¡Y la marmota parió un escribano con pluma y tintero de cuerno, en la mano! Y el escribano parió un escribiente con pluma y tintero de cuerno, en la frente!

EL FANTOCHE: ¡Calla, renegado perro de Moisés! Tú buscas morir degollado por mi cuchillo portugués.

---

1 A political boss and election-rigger who had enormous influence and powers of patronage, especially in rural towns.

STRAPHALARIUS: Exactly. And the very same thing happens with anything that amuses us; we only make a joke out of those things on the same level as ourselves.

IMMANUEL: But we are obliged to love, Straphalarius. Laughter and tears are the way of the Lord. That's my philosophy of art and yours as well.

STRAPHALARIUS: It's not mine. My aesthetics are a transcending of laughter and pain, like the conversations dead people must have when they tell stories about the living.

IMMANUEL: What leads you to believe the stories of the dead are like that?

STRAPHALARIUS: Because they're no longer mortal. All art is inspired by the realisation that one day we will all pass on. That piece of knowledge makes men more equal than the French Revolution ever did.

IMMANUEL: You want to be like God, Straphalarius!

STRAPHALARIUS: I'd like to look upon this world with the same perspective as those on the other shore. I'm like that relative of mine you once met who, when he was asked one day by the boss what he wanted to be, replied: "Me? Deceased!"

In the yard of the inn, under the cover of awnings, a group of fair-goers has got together. Beneath the brown cloak of a wily old-timer can be seen the shapes of puppets of a rudimentary, popular theatre. The showman fingers a fandango on his battered hurdy-gurdy and his apprentice, a lad full of tricks, hides himself under the cloak to work the puppets. The performance begins.

SHOWMAN: Mr Punch, Lieutenant Sir, let's have your head out here in the air!

VOICE OF PUPPET: I'm on guard duty in the barracks.

SHOWMAN: Bollocks to your barracks! Your piece of crumpet, Lieutenant Sir, is getting some extra drill.

VOICE OF PUPPET: It's a lie!

SHOWMAN: No lies will he tell, not Blind Fidel.

The puppet, his arms flung out in a cross and his kepi over his ear, appears on the shoulder of his old sidekick, who winks an eye at him and sings along to his hurdy-gurdy.

SHOWMAN: To my hey to my ho, to my merry little dancer,
          For sweet Saint Lilaila's given birth to a hamster;
          And the hamster has gone and given birth to a lawyer
          With a quill and a pen made of horn in his drawer.
          To the wife of the lawyer a clerk has been born
          And adorning his brow are the pens made of horn!

PUPPET: Shut your gob, you filthy Jewish dog! You're after getting your throat slit by my Portuguese chopper!

EL BULULU ¡Sooo! No camine tan agudo, mi Teniente Don Friolera, y mate usted a la bolichera, si no se aviene con ser cornudo.

EL FANTOCHE: ¡Repara, Fidel, que no soy su marido, y al no serlo no puedo ser juez!

EL BULULU: Pues será usted un cabrón consentido.

EL FANTOCHE: Antes que eso le pico la nuez. ¿Quién mi honra escarnece?

EL BULULU: Pedro Mal-Casado.

EL FANTOCHE: ¿Qué pena merece?

EL BULULU: Morir degollado.

EL FANTOCHE: ¿En qué oficio trata?

EL BULULU: Burros aceiteros conduce en reata, ganando dineros. Mi Teniente Don Friolera, llame usted a la bolichera.

EL FANTOCHE: ¡Comparece, mujer deshonesta!

UN GRITO CHILLON: ¿Amor mío, por qué así me injurias?

EL FANTOCHE: ¡A este puñal pide respuesta!

EL GRITO CHILLON: ¡Amor mío, calma tus furias!

Por el otro hombro del compadre, hace su aparición una moña, cara de luna y pelo de estopa: en el rodete una rosa de papel. Grita aspando los brazos. Manotea. Se azota con rabioso tableteo la cara de madera.

EL BULULU: Si la camisa de la bolichera huele a aceite, mátela usted.

LA MOÑA: ¡Ciego piojoso, no encismes a un hombre celoso!

EL BULULU: Si pringa de aceite, dele usted mulé. Levántele usted el refajo, sáquele usted el faldón para fuera, y olisquee a qué huele el pispajo, mi Teniente Don Friolera. ¿Mi Teniente, que dice el faldón?

EL FANTOCHE: ¡Válgame Dios, que soy un cabrón!

EL BULULU: Dele usted, mi Teniente, baqueta. Zúrrela usted, mi Teniente, el pandero. Ábrala usted con la bayoneta, en la pelleja, un agujero. ¡Mátela usted si huele a aceitero!

LA MOÑA: Vertióseme anoche el candil al meterme en los cobertores. ¡De eso me huele el fogaril, no de andar en otros amores! ¡Ciego mentiroso, mira tú de no ser más cabrón, y no encismes el corazón de un enamorado celoso!

EL BULULU: ¡Ande usted, mi Teniente, con ella! ¡Cósala usted con un puñal! Tiene usted, por su buena estrella, vecina la raya de Portugal.

EL FANTOCHE: ¡Me comeré en albondiguillas el tasajo de esta bribona, y haré de su sangre morcillas!

EL BULULU: Convide usted a la comilona.

LA MOÑA: ¡Derramas mi sangre inocente, cruel enamorado! ¡No dicta sentencia el hombre prudente, por murmuraciones de un malvado!

SHOWMAN: Hold your horses! Let's not be so hasty, Mr Punch! See your
　　　　　Judy off, Lieutenant Sir, if being a cuckold sends you so spare!
PUPPET: Look here, Fidel; I'm not her husband and, for that reason, I can't be
　　　　her judge.
SHOWMAN: All right then, you'll be a consenting cuckold.
PUPPET: I'll have her guts for garters first! And who is it that's knocking
　　　　lumps off my honour?
SHOWMAN: Peter Put-it-about.
PUPPET: And what does he deserve?
SHOWMAN: His gizzard ripping out.
PUPPET: What trade does he serve?
SHOWMAN: He drives a mule-train selling oil for a wage. Mr Punch,
　　　　　Lieutenant Sir, order your floozie out here on the stage.
PUPPET: Let's be having you, you faithless woman!
A SCREECH: My love, why do you wrong me so?
PUPPET: Ask this dagger the answer to that!
THE SCREECH: For pity's sake, temper your rage!

*On the old man's other shoulder appears a doll with a moon-like face and burlap
hair. In her hair-bun there is a paper rose. She gesticulates and flails her arms as
she shouts, striking her wooden face with a furious clatter.*

SHOWMAN: If your Judy's shirt smells of oil, then bump her off!
DOLL: Don't stir up the passions of a jealous man, you blind old flea-bag!
SHOWMAN: If there's a whiff of oil, then give her what for! Lift up her skirt-
　　　　　tails, whip out her shift and have a sniff of the smell of the rag.
　　　　　Mr Punch, Lieutenant Sir,what is the tale the skirt's got to tell?
PUPPET: It says I'm a cuckold, oh bloody hell!
SHOWMAN: Do her in proper, Lieutenant Sah! Smash up her face till it looks
　　　　　like a doily! Rip out her guts for acting so coyly! Stab her to
　　　　　death if she smells at all oily!
DOLL: The oil-lamp spilled on me last night as I got under the covers. That's
　　　　the reason my stoke-hole smells, not from having other lovers!
　　　　You lying old fart! Don't be a bigger twat than you already are
　　　　and don't go inciting a jealous man's heart!
SHOWMAN: Come on, Lieutenant, give her what for! Stitch her up with your
　　　　　knife! It's your lucky day, 'cause the Portuguese border's not far
　　　　　away.
PUPPET: I'll make meat-balls out of her guts and use her blood to make black
　　　　puddings!
SHOWMAN: You must invite me to the nosh-up.
DOLL: It's innocent blood you spill, oh cruel lover! No sensible man would
　　　　find me guilty merely on the word of a scoundrel!

EL FANTOCHE: ¡Muere, ingrata! ¡Guiña el ojo y estira la pata!

LA MOÑA: ¡Muerta soy! ¡El Teniente me mata!

El fantoche reparte tajos y cuchilladas con la cimitarra de Otelo. La corva hoja reluce terrible sobre la cabeza del compadre. La moña cae soltando las horquillas y enseñando las calcetas. Remolino de gritos y brazos aspados.

EL BULULU: ¡Mi Teniente, alerta, que con los fusiles están los civiles llamando a la puerta! ¡Del Burgo, Cabrejas, Medina y Valduero, las cuatro parejas, con el aceitero!

EL FANTOCHE: ¡San Cristo, que apuro!

EL BULULU: Al pie de la muerta, suene usted, mi Teniente, un duro por ver si despierta. ¿Mi Teniente, cómo responde?

EL FANTOCHE: ¿Cómo responde? Con una higa,[1] y el duro esconde bajo la liga.

EL BULULU: Mi Teniente, es alta la media?

EL FANTOCHE: ¡Si es alta la media! Media conejera.[2]

EL BULULU: ¡Olé la Trigedia de los Cuernos de Don Friolera!

Termina la representación. Aire de fandango en la zanfoña del compadre. El acólito deja el socaire de la capa, y da vuelta al corro, haciendo saltar cuatro perronas en un platillo de peltre. En lo alto del mirador, las cabezas vascongadas sonríen ingenuamente.

DON MANOLITO: Parece teatro napolitano.

DON ESTRAFALARIO: Pudiera acaso ser latino. Indudablemente la comprensión de este humor y esta moral, no es de tradición castellana. Es portuguesa y cántabra, y tal vez de la montaña de Cataluña. Las otras regiones, literariamente, no saben nada de estas burlas de cornudos, y este donoso buen sentido, tan contrario al honor teatral y africano de Castilla. Ese tabanque de muñecos sobre la espalda de un viejo prosero, para mí, es más sugestivo que todo el retórico teatro español. Y no digo esto por amor a las formas populares de la literatura ... ¡Ahí están las abominables coplas de Joselito!

---

1   Literally, a fig. Apart from being an allusion to the female sexual organ, the word was also contemporary slang for the rude gesture of inserting the thumb between the index and second finger of the closed hand.

2   Literally, rabbit-net stocking. *Conejo* also has the additional obscene meaning of 'pussy' (as its English equivalent 'coney' once had).

PUPPET: Die, you ingrate, my love you besmirch! Curl up your tootsies and
        fall off your perch!
DOLL: Murder! Murder! The Lieutenant's killing me!

*The Puppet stabs and slashes with Othello's scimitar, its curved blade flashing
dreadfully above the blind man's head. The Doll falls backwards, her stockings
showing and her hair-grips falling loose. A swirl of screams and a flailing of
arms.*

SHOWMAN: Be on your guard, Lieutenant Sir, the Civil Guard are banging
         below on the door! Each town in the province has sent in a pair;
         they're with the oil-trader at the foot of the stair!
PUPPET: Holy cow, but I'm in for it now!
SHOWMAN: Lieutenant, jangle a shilling at your dead Judy's ear to see if she'll
         revive. What's her answer, Sir?
PUPPET: What's her answer? A wide open member – and she's hidden the
        shilling in her suspender!
SHOWMAN: Lieutenant, do her stockings go up high?
PUPPET: Do her stockings go up high? They go right up to her raspberry pie!
SHOWMAN: So ends the trudgedy of Mr Punch The Cuckold! [1]

*The performance ends. The puppeteer plays a fandango on his hurdy-gurdy. His
apprentice leaves the cover of his cape and returns to the yard, jangling a few
coppers on a pewter plate. Above, in the balcony, the Basque heads smile
ingenuously.*

IMMANUEL: It reminds me of Neapolitan theatre.
STRAPHALARIUS: It could almost be Latin. There's no doubt that the
          understanding shown by this humour and sense of morality has
          no part in the Castilian tradition. It's Portuguese and Cantabrian
          in essence, or perhaps also from the foothills of Catalonia. As for
          the other regions of Spain, they've no idea about this kind of
          cuckold-mockery and its good-humoured common sense. It's the
          very opposite of the African and theatrical honour typical of
          Castile. This treadle of dolls on an old Punch-and-Judy man's
          shoulders is, for me, more suggestive than the Spanish theatre
          and all its rhetoric. And I'm not saying that out of love of popular
          forms of literature – just look at those abominable ballads about
          Joselito the bullfighter.

---

1 The wilful mispronunciation serves to emphasise the anti-tragic, skittish flavour
   of Blind Fidel's treatment of the Othello tale.

DON MANOLITO: A usted le gustan las del Espartero.

DON ESTRFALARIO: Todas son abominables. Don Manolito, cada cual tiene el poeta que se merece.

DON MANOLITO: Las otras notabilidades nacionales no pasan de la gacetilla.

DON ESTRAFALARIO: Esas coplas de toreros, asesinos y ladrones, son periodismo ramplón.

DON MANOLITO: Usted, con ser tan sabio, las juzga por lectura, y de ahí no pasa. ¡Pero cuando se cantan con acompañamiento de guitarra, adquieren una gran emoción! No me negará usted que el romance de ciego, hiperbólico, truculento y sanguinario, es una forma popular.

DON ESTRAFALARIO: Una forma popular judaica, como el honor calderoniano. La crueldad y el dogmatismo del drama español solamente se encuentra en la Bilbia. La crueldad sespiriana es magnífica, porque es ciega, con la grandeza de las fuerzas naturales. Shakespeare es violento, pero no dogmático. La crueldad española tiene toda la bárbara liturgia de los Autos de Fe. Es fría y antipática. Nada más lejos de la furia ciega de los elementos que Torquemada: es una furia escolástica. Si nuestro teatro tuviese el temblor de las fiestas de toros, sería magnífico. Si hubiese sabido transportar esa violencia estética, sería un teatro heroico como la Ilíada. A falta de eso, tiene toda la antipatía de los códigos, desde la Constitución a la Gramática.

DON MANOLITO: Porque usted es anarquista.

DON ESTRAFALARIO: ¡Tal vez!

DON MANOLITO: ¿Y de dónde nos vendrá la redención, Don Estrafalario?

DON ESTRAFALARIO: Del compadre Fidel. ¡Don Manolito, el retablo de este tuno vale más que su Orbaneja!

DON MANOLITO: ¿Por qué?

DON ESTRAFALARIO: Está más lleno de posibilidades.

DON MANOLITO: No admito esa respuesta. Usted no es filósofo, y no tiene derecho a responderme con pedanterías. Usted no es más que hereje, como Don Miguel de Unamuno.

IMMANUEL: You prefer those about Espartero[1], instead.

STRAPHALARIUS: They're all abominable. The people, Immanuel, get the
poets they deserve.

IMMANUEL: Anything else the nation has of note is no better than the
scrawlings in the gossip columns.

STRAPHALARIUS: All those ballads about bullfighters, murderers and thieves
are just so much gutter journalism.

IMMANUEL: Ah but you, because you're so learned, judge them as reading
material and take it no further. When they're recited to guitar
accompaniment they become intensely moving! You can hardly
deny that the traditional street-ballad, so blood-thirsty, garish and
exaggerated, is, nevertheless, a popular form.

STRAPHALARIUS: A Judaic popular form, like Calderón and his treatment of
honour. The cruelty and dogmatism of Spanish drama comes
straight from the Bible. Shakespearian cruelty is magnificent
because it's blind, with all the greatness of the forces of Nature.
Shakespeare is violent but never dogmatic. Spanish cruelty has
all the barbarous liturgy of an *auto-da-fe*. It's cold and repugnant.
There's nothing further from the fury of the elements than
Torquemada[2]. It's a scholastic fury. If our theatre had the vibrancy
of the bullfight it would be magnificent. If it had managed to
transpose that aesthetic of violence, it would have been heroic
like the Iliad. But since it's never managed to do this, it has the
coldness of every set of rules from the Spanish Constitution to
the standard school grammar.

IMMANUEL: Only because you're an anarchist.

STRAPHALARIUS: Maybe!

IMMANUEL: And where will our redemption come from, Straphalarius?

STRAPHALARIUS: From Blind Fidel. Immanuel, this crafty old-timer's show
is far more valuable than that painting of yours.

IMMANUEL: Why?

STRAPHALARIUS: It has far more possibilities.

IMMANUEL: I'm not having that. You're no philosopher and you've got no
right to be pedantic with me. You're nothing more than a heretic,
like Miguel de Unamuno[3].

---

1 Both of these street-ballads deal with the death (in the arena) of famous
bullfighters, but whereas the verses inspired by Joselito (José Gómez Ortega)
were of recent origin (he was killed in 1920), those recounting the fate of
Espartero (Manuel García Cuesta) would have been in currency since 1894.

2 Tomás de Torquemada (1420-98), a fanatical Dominican priest who instigated the
procedural rigour and cruelty of the Spanish Inquisition.

3 The contemporary Spanish philosopher (1864-1936) was well known for his
rejection of comfortable orthodoxies.

DON ESTRAFALARIO: ¡A Dios gracias! Pero alguna vez hay que ser pedante. El compadre Fidel es superior a Yago. Yago, cuando desata aquel conflicto de celos, quiere vengarse, mientras que ese otro tuno, espíritu mucho más cultivado, sólo trata de divertirse a costa de Don Friolera. Shakespeare rima con el latido de su corazón, el corazón de Otelo. Se desdobla en los celos del Moro; creador y criatura son del mismo barro humano. En tanto ese Bululú, ni un solo momento deja de considerarse superior, por naturaleza, a los muñecos de su tabanque. Tiene una dignidad demiúrgica.

DON MANOLITO: Lo que usted echaba de menos en el Diablo de mi Orbaneja.

DON ESTRAFALARIO: Cabalmente, alma de Dios.

DON MANOLITO: ¿Qué haría usted viendo ahorcarse a un pecador?

DON ESTRAFALARIO: Preguntarle por qué no lo había hecho antes. El Diablo es un intelectual, un filósofo, en su significación etimológica de amor y saber. El Deseo de Conocimiento se llama Diablo.

DON MANOLITO: El Diablo de usted es demasiado universitario.

DON ESTRAFALARIO: Fue estudiante en Maguncia e inventó allí el arte funesto de la Imprenta.

STRAPHALARIUS: Thanks be to God! But from time to time you've got to be pedantic. Blind Fidel is superior to Iago. Iago, when he unleashes the great forces of jealousy, is out for revenge, whereas our other rogue, a far more refined old soul, is only out to have a laugh at Mr Punch's expense. Shakespeare puts Othello's heart in tune with his own. He opens himself up to the jealousy felt by the Moor. Creator and creature are both made of the same human clay.This puppeteer, however, at no time considers himself anything but superior in nature to the puppets in his show. He has a demiurgic type of dignity.

IMMANUEL: Which was what you found lacking in the Devil in my painting.

STRAPHALARIUS: Precisely, dear heart.

IMMANUEL: But what would you do if you came across some poor sinner trying to hang himself?

STRAPHALARIUS: Ask him why he hadn't got round to it sooner. The Devil is an intellectual, a philosopher, in the etymological meaning of love and knowledge. The desire for knowledge is what we call the Devil.

IMMANUEL: This Devil of yours sounds too academic for my liking.

STRAPHALARIUS: He was a student in Mainz and there he invented the ominous device of the printing-press.

Escena primera

San Fernando de Cabo Estrivel: una ciudad empingorotada sobre cantiles. En los cristales de los miradores, el sol enciende los mismos cabrilleos que en la turquesa del mar. A lo largo de los muelles, un mecerse de arboladuras, velámenes y chimeneas. En la punta, estremecida por bocanadas de aire, la garita del Resguardo. Olor de caña quemada. Olor de tabaco. Olor de brea. Levante fresco. El himno inglés en las remotas cornetas de un barco de guerra. A la puerta de la garita, con el fusil terciado, un carabinero, y en el marco azul del ventanillo, la gorra de cuartel, una oreja y la pipa del Teniente don Pascual Astete "Don Friolera". Una sombra, raposa, cautelosa, ronda la garita. Por el ventanillo asesta una piedra y escapa agachada. La piedra trae atado un papel con un escrito. Don Friolera lo recoge turulato, y espanta los ojos leyendo el papel.

DON FRIOLERA: Tu mujer piedra de escándalo. ¡Esto es un rayo a mis pies! ¡Loreta con sentencia de muerte! ¡Friolera! ¡Si fuese verdad tendría que degollarla! ¡Irremisiblemente condenada! En el Cuerpo de Carabineros no hay cabrones. ¡Friolera! Y ¿quién será el carajuelo que le ha trastornado los cascos a esa Putifar? ... Afortunadamente no pasará de una vil calumnia. Este pueblo es un pueblo de canallas. Pero hay que andarse con pupila. A Loreta me la solivianta ese pendejo de Pachequín. Ya me tenía la mosca en la oreja. Caer, no ha caído. ¡Friolera! Si supiese que vainípedo escribió este papel, se lo comía. Para algunos canallas no hay mujer honrada ... Solicitaré el traslado por si tiene algún fundamento esta infame calumnia ... Cualquier ligereza, una imprudencia, las mujeres no reflexionan. ¡Pueblo de canallas! Yo no me divorcio por una denuncia anónima. ¡La desprecio! Loreta seguirá siendo mi compañera, el ángel de mi hogar. Nos casamos enamorados, y eso nunca se olvida. Matrimonio de ilusión. Matrimonio de puro amor. ¡Friolera!

Se enternece contemplando un guardapelo colgante en la cadena del reloj, suspira y enjuga una lágrima. Pasa por su voz el trémolo de un sollozo, y se le arruga la voz, con las mismas arrugas que la cara.

Scene One

San Fernando de Cabo Estrivel: a town perched out on steep rocks. Dancing on the window panes are those same reflections that the sun lights upon the turquoise of the sea. Along the quayside, a swaying of masts, sails and funnels. At the far point, shaken by gusts of wind, the guard hut of the Customs House. The smell of burnt grog. The smell of tobacco. The smell of tar. Fresh east wind. The English national anthem on the distant cornets of a warship. Outside the guard hut, a soldier, his rifle slung diagonally, and in the blue frame of the little window, the forage cap, ear and pipe of Lieutenant Don Pascual Astete – Mr Punch -. A cunning, cautious shadow creeps round the sentry box. It throws a stone through the window and steals away in a crouch. Attached to the stone is a piece of paper with a message. Gob-smacked, Mr Punch picks it up and his eyes show horror as he reads.

MR PUNCH: Your wife a source of scandal. What a thunderbolt at my door! Loretta under sentence of death! Oh deary, deary me! If this were true, I'd have to slit her throat! Guilty without leave to appeal! They don't allow cuckolds in the Customs Corps. Oh deary, deary me! I just wonder who's the bloody stud that turned the head of that little Judy of mine ... Thank God it's nothing more than malicious rumour. Town full of shits! But I'll have to watch my step. My little Loretta's been sweet-talked by that poltroonly little Pacheco. I've always had my suspicions about that. But as for succumbing, I'm sure she's not succumbed yet! Deary, deary me! If I only knew what creep has written this, I'd push it right back down his throat. For some shits there's no such thing as a decent woman ... I'll put in for a transfer just in case this vile slander has any basis in fact ... The merest flightiness, the slightest indiscretion, women don't bear these things in mind. Town full of shits! I'm not going to get divorced just because of an anonymous tip-off. I've nothing but contempt for it! Loretta will continue to be my wife, the angel of my home. We married for love and that's not something you can forget, ever. A marriage full of hopes, full of pure love. Oh deary, deary me!

He mellows as he gazes upon a locket hanging from his watch-chain. He sighs as he wipes away a tear. Through his voice slips the trembling of a sob. His voice wrinkles, with the self-same wrinkles as those on his face.

DON FRIOLERA: ¿Y si esta infamia fuese verdad? La mujer es frágil. ¿Quién le iba con el soplo al Teniente Capriles? ... ¡Friolera! ¡Y era público que su esposa le coronaba! No era un cabrón consentido. No lo era ... Se lo achacaban. Y cuando lo supo mató como un héroe a la mujer, al asistente y al gato. Amigos de toda la vida. Compañeros de campaña. Los dos con la Medalla de Joló. Estábamos llamados a una suerte pareja. El oficial pundonoroso, jamás perdona a la esposa adúltera. Es una barbaridad. Para muchos lo es. Yo no lo admito. A la mujer que sale mala, pena capital. El paisano, y el propio oficial retirado, en algunas ocasiones, muy contadas, pueden perdonar. Se dan circunstancias. La mujer que violan contra su voluntad, la que atropellan acostada durmiendo, la mareada con alguna bebida. Solamente en estos casos admito yo la caída de Loreta. Y en estos casos tampoco podría perdonarla. Sirvo en activo. Pudiera hacerlo retirado del servicio. ¡Friolera!

Vuelve a deletrear con las cejas torcidas sobre el papel. Lo escudriña al trasluz, se lo pasa por la nariz, olfateando. Al cabo lo pliega y esconde en el fondo de la petaca.

DON FRIOLERA: ¡Mi mujer piedra de escándalo! El torcedor ya lo tengo. Si es verdad, quisiera no haberlo sabido. Me reconozco un calzonazos. ¿Adónde voy yo con mis cincuenta y tres años averiados? ¡Una vida rota! En qué poco está la felicidad, en que la mujer te salga cabra. ¡Qué mal ángel, destruir con una denuncia anónima la paz conyugal! ¡Canallas! De buena gana quisiera atrapar una enfermedad y morirme en tres días. ¡Soy un mandria! ¡A mis años andar a tiros! ... ¿Y si cerrase los ojos para ese contrabando? ¿Y si resolviese no saber nada? ¡Este mundo es una solfa! ¿Qué culpa tiene el marido de que la mujer le salga rana? ¡Y no basta una honrosa separación! ¡Friolera! ¡Si bastase! ... La galería no se conforma con eso. El principio del honor ordena matar. ¡Pim! ¡Pam! ¡Pum! ... El mundo nunca se cansa de ver títeres y agradece

MR PUNCH: But just suppose this infamy were true? Women are so frail. Who was it blew the gaff to Lieutenant Hornblower? ... Deary, deary me! And it was public knowledge that his wife was doing the dirty on him. He was no consenting cuckold, though, not him! ... But that's what they accused him of. And when he found out, he killed his wife, his batman and the cat. A real hero! Lifelong friends and all! Brothers-in-arms, him and me. Both of us with the Jolo[1] medal. And now the pair of us summoned by the self-same fate. The honour-bound officer can never forgive his adulterous wife. It's barbaric, at least there's many say it is. But I'm not having that. For the wife who goes crook on you the penalty is death! Civilians and even retired officers may, on very few occasions, find themselves in a position where they're able to forgive. There may be some extenuating circumstance: a woman who's been raped, against her will; one who's knocked off in bed, asleep; the woman who's tiddly after a drink or two. It would only be in this type of case that I could accept Loretta's misdemeanour. But even in such an instance I could never forgive her. I'm on active service. I could do it if I was back in Civvy Street. Deary, deary me!

His eyebrows twisted over the note, he scrutinises it once more. He holds it up to the light, he runs it under his nose and sniffs it. In the end, he folds it up and hides it deep in his pouch.

MR PUNCH: My wife a source of scandal! This has really screwed me up. If it is true, I'd rather not have known. What a wimp I've always been! And where do I go from here, fifty-three years old and my life in ruins? How fleeting happiness is! It lasts only until your wife goes crook on you. What a dirty trick, destroying conjugal bliss with an anonymous tip-off! Shithouses! If I could only catch some disease and be dead within three days. Oh I am a cowardy custard, but I can't go round shooting people – not at my age! ... Just suppose I turned a blind eye to this under-the-counter dealing and made up my mind to look the other way? This world is a bed of nails! How is a husband to blame if his wife turns out to be a bad'un? And a decent separation just isn't good enough! Deary, deary me! If only it were! ... But yer public opinion won't settle for that. The honour principle demands the shedding of blood. Bang! Bang! Bang! That's the way to do it! ... People never get

---

1 Part of the Philippines, where the Spanish army had been engaged in containing a national independence movement before the colony was lost to the United States in 1898.

el espectáculo de balde. ¡Formulismos! ... ¡Bastante tiene con su pena el ciudadano que ve deshecha su casa! ¡Ya lo creo! La mujer por un camino, el marido por otro, los hijos sin calor, desamparados. Y al sujeto, en estas circunstancias, le piden que degüelle y se satisfaga con sangre, como si no tuviese otra cosa que rencor en el alma. ¡Friolera! Y todos somos unos botarates. Yo mataré como el primero. ¡Friolera! Soy un militar español y no tengo derecho a filosofar como en Francia. ¡En el Cuerpo de Carabineros no hay maridos cabrones! ¡Friolera!

Acalorado, se quita el gorro y mete la cabeza por el ventanillo, respirando en las ráfagas del mar. Los cuatro pelos de su calva bailan un baile fatuo. En el fondo del muelle, sobre un grupo de mujeres y rapaces, bambolea el ataúd destinado a un capitán mercante, fallecido a bordo de su barco. Pachequín el barbero, que fue llamado para rajarle las barbas, cojea detrás, pisándose la punta de la capa. Don Friolera, al verle, se recoge en la garita. Le tiembla el bigote como a los gatos cuando estornudan.

DON FRIOLERA: ¡Era feliz sin saberlo, y ha venido ese pata coja a robarme la dicha! ... Y acaso no ... Esta sospecha debo desecharla. ¿Qué fundamento tiene? ¡Ninguno! ¡El canalla que escribió el anónimo es el verdadero canalla! Si esa calumnia fuese verdad, ateo como soy, falto de los consuelos religiosos, náufrago en la vida ... En estas ocasiones, sin un amigo con quien manifestarse y alguna creencia, el hombre lo pasa mal. ¡Amigo! ¡No hay amigos! ¡Tú eres un ejemplo, Juanito Pacheco!

Cambia el gorro por el ros y sale de la garita. El carabinero de la puerta se cuadra, y el teniente le mira enigmático.

DON FRIOLERA: ¿Qué haría usted si le engañase su mujer, Cabo Alegría?
EL CARABINERO: Mi Teniente, matarla como manda Dios.
DON FRIOLERA: ¡Y después!
EL CARABINERO: ¡Después, pedir el traslado!

tired of puppet-shows and love watching the spectacle free, gratis
and for nothing! Bleeding social norms! ... Hasn't your average
bloke got enough on his plate seeing his home falling to pieces? I
ask you! His missus off one way and him off another, with the
children left cold, hungry and destitute. And in circumstances like
these they ask a man to go round slitting throats to satisfy his
honour with blood, as if he had nothing more in his soul than
bitterness. Oh deary, deary me! We go right over the top, the lot
of us. And so I'll go off and murder, just like the next man.
Deary, deary me! I am a Spanish officer and haven't got the right
to philosophise like they do in France. Cuckolds aren't allowed in
the Customs Corps! Oh deary, deary me!

*Flushed, he takes off his cap and pokes his head out of the window, breathing in
the sea air. The few hairs left on his head dance a will-o'-the-wisp dance. At the
end of the quay, on the shoulders of a group of women and youths, bobs the
coffin of a captain in the Merchant Navy who died aboard ship. Pachequín, the
barber, summoned to scrape off his whiskers, limps along behind, treading on
the end of his cape. Mr Punch, seeing him, retreats into his office. His
moustache quivers like the whiskers of cats when they sneeze.*

MR PUNCH: I was happy and I didn't know it, and now that sod with the
             gammy leg has come along to steal all my happiness! ... Though
             maybe not ... Strike that suspicion from the record. What basis in
             fact has it got? None whatsoever! Whoever wrote that note's the
             real shit! If that piece of slander were true, atheist that I am and
             deprived of any religious comfort, I'd be shipwrecked in this life
             ... It's at moments like this, with no faith left in anyone or
             anything, that a man really knows just what a bad time is!
             Friends? There's no such thing as friends! And you're the proof of
             that, Johnny Pacheco!

*He changes his cap for his kepi and leaves the office. The sentry outside comes
to attention and the Lieutenant looks at him enigmatically.*

MR PUNCH: Corporal Jolly, what would you do if your wife was unfaithful to
             you?
CARABINEER: Do my Christian duty, sir, and kill her.
MR PUNCH: And what would you do after that?
CARABINEER: What would I do after that? Put in for a transfer!

40

Escena segunda

Costanilla de Santiago el Verde, subiendo del puerto. Casas encaladas, patios floridos, morunos canceles. Juanito Pacheco, Pachequín el barbero, cuarentón cojo y narigudo, con capa torera y quepis azul, rasguea la guitarra sentado bajo el jaulote de la cotorra, chillón y cromático. Doña Loreta, la señora tenienta, en la reja de una casa fronteriza, se prende un clavel en el rodete. Pachequín canta con los ojos en blanco.

PACHEQUIN: A tus pies, gachona mía,
            pongo todo mi caudal:
            Una jaca terciopelo,
            un trabuco y un puñal ...

LA COTORRA: ¡Olé! ¡Viva tu madre!
DOÑA LORETA: ¡Hasta la cotorra le jalea a usted, Pachequín!
PACHEQUIN: ¡Tiene un gusto muy refinado!
DOÑA LORETA: Le adula.
PACHEQUIN: No sea usted satírica, Doña Loreta. Concédame que algo se
           chanela.
DOÑA LORETA: ¿Qué toma usted para tener esa voz perlada?
PACHEQUIN: Rejalgares[1] que me da una vecina muy flamenca.
DOÑA LORETA: Serán rejalgares, pero a usted se le convierten en jarabe de
           pico.
PACHEQUIN: ¡Usted no me ha oído suspirar! ¡Pues va a ser preciso que usted
           me oiga!
DOÑA LORETA: Me he quedado sorda de un aire.
PACHEQUIN: Son rejalgares, Doña Loreta.
DOÑA LORETA: Pero no los recibirá usted de mano de vecina, pues toda la
           tarde se la pasó el amigo de bureo.
PACHEQUIN: Le debo una explicación, Doña Loreta.
DOÑA LORETA: ¡Qué miramiento! ¡A mí no me debe usted nada!
PACHEQUIN: Han reclamado mis servicios para rapar las barbas de un muerto.
DOÑA LORETA: ¡Mala sombra!
PACHEQUIN: Un servidor no cree en agüeros. Falleció a bordo el capitán de la
           Joven Pepita.
DOÑA LORETA: ¡Por eso hacía señal la campana de Santiago el Verde!
PACHEQUIN: A las siete es el sepelio.
DOÑA LORETA: ¿Falleció de su muerte?

---

1 Sulphur of arsenic. *Dar rejalgares* was a popular expression for turning down
    amorous advances.

Scene Two

A steep, narrow street winding up from the harbour to Santiago el Verde. Whitewashed houses, patios with flowering plants, Moorish-style gates. Johnny Pacheco, Pachequín the Barber, a long-nosed man in his forties with a limp, wearing a bullfighter-style cape and a blue military cap, is strumming a guitar as he sits beneath a large cage containing a multi-hued, screeching parrot. Loretta, the Lieutenant's wife, standing at the grille of a house opposite, is fastening a carnation in her hair-bun. Pachequín sings, rolling his eyes.

PACHEQUIN: At your feet, my enchantress,
        my fortune I lay down:
        a glossy-coated pony,
        a dagger and a gun.
THE PARROT: Olé! Who's a pretty boy!
LORETTA: Even the parrot's applauding you, Pachequín!
PACHEQUIN: He's got very refined taste!
LORETTA: He's just buttering you up.
PACHEQUIN: Don't be so sarcastic, Loretta. You might at least admit I know
        a thing or two when it comes to singing.
LORETTA: What have you been knocking back to put you in such exquisite
        voice?
PACHEQUIN: It's me that's been knocked back, by a certain neighbour of
        mine, a real gypsy charmer.
LORETTA: You're getting no joy out of me, right enough, but it doesn't seem
        to stop your sweet-talking.
PACHEQUIN: If only you'd heard me sighing for love! This time you've got to
        listen to me!
LORETTA: Can't hear a word you're saying.
PACHEQUIN: Cruelly spurned, Loretta!
LORETTA: But not by any woman here, my friend, because you've been off on
        a spree all afternoon.
PACHEQUIN: I owe you an explanation, Loretta.
LORETTA: Such delicacy! You don't owe me a thing!
PACHEQUIN: My services were required to shave a corpse.
LORETTA: That's a bad omen!
PACHEQUIN: Yours truly doesn't believe in omens. The captain of the *Young
        Pepita* died on board his ship.
LORETTA: So that's why the church bell of Santiago el Verde was tolling!
PACHEQUIN: The funeral is at seven.
LORETTA: Did he die a natural death?

PACHEQUIN: Falleció de unas calenturas, y lo propio del marino es morir ahogado.

DOÑA LORETA: Y lo propio de un barbero, morir de pelmazo.

PACHEQUIN: ¡Doña Loreta, es usted más rica que una ciruela!

DOÑA LORETA: Y usted un vivales.

PACHEQUIN: Yo un pipi sin papeles, que está por usted ventolera.

DOÑA LORETA: ¡Que se busca usted un compromiso con mi esposo!

PACHEQUIN: Ya andaríamos con pupila, llegado el caso, Doña Loreta.

DOÑA LORETA: No hay pecado sellado.

PACHEQUIN: ¿Y de saberse, qué haría el Teniente?

DOÑA LORETA: ¡Matarnos!

PACHEQUIN: No llame usted a esa puerta tan negra. ¡Sería un por de mas!

DOÑA LORETA: ¡Ay, Pachequín, la esposa del militar, si cae, ya sabe lo que la espera!

PACHEQUIN: ¿No le agradaría a usted morir como una celebridad, y que su retrato saliese en la prensa?

DOÑA LORETA: ¡La vida es muy rica, Pachequín! A mí me va muy bien en ella.

PACHEQUIN: ¿Es posible que no le camele a usted salir retratada en el ABC?[1]

DOÑA LORETA: ¡Tío guasa!

PACHEQUIN: ¿Quiere decirse que le es a usted inverosímil?

DOÑA LORETA: ¡Completamente!

PACHEQUIN: No paso a creerlo.

DOÑA LORETA: Como sus murgas esta servidora.

PACHEQUIN: No es caso parejo. ¿Qué prueba de amor me pide usted, Doña Loreta?

DOÑA LORETA: Ninguna. Tenga usted juicio y no me sofoque.

PACHEQUIN: ¿Va usted a quererme?

DOÑA LORETA: Ha hecho usted muchas picardías en el mundo, y pudiera suceder que las pagase todas juntas.

PACHEQUIN: Si había de aplicarme usted el castigo, lo celebraría.

DOÑA LORETA: Usted se olvida de mi esposo.

PACHEQUIN: Quiérame usted, que para ese toro tengo yo la muleta de Juan Belmonte.

DOÑA LORETA: No puedo quererle, Pachequín.

PACHEQUIN: ¿Y tampoco puede usted darme el clavel que luce en el moño?

DOÑA LORETA: ¿Me va mal?

PACHEQUIN: Le irá a usted mejor este reventón de mi solapa. ¿Cambiamos?

---

1 A daily paper of markedly conservative and monarchist sympathies.

PACHEQUIN: He died of a fever, and the fitting end for a sailor is drowning.

LORETTA: And the fitting end for a barber is boring himself to death.

PACHEQUIN: Loretta, what a juicy little plum you are!

LORETTA: And you're just trying it on.

PACHEQUIN: Me, I'm just a poor little squaddie who's crazy about you.

LORETTA: You're heading for trouble with my husband!

PACHEQUIN: If it came to it, we'd keep a sharp look-out, Loretta.

LORETTA: Sin will always out.

PACHEQUIN: And supposing we were found out, what could the Lieutenant do?

LORETTA: Kill us!

PACHEQUIN: Don't even think such a terrible thing. That would be going too far!

LORETTA: Oh, Pachequín, if a soldier's wife steps out of line she knows what's in store for her!

PACHEQUIN: Wouldn't you be pleased if your death made you famous and your picture came out in the Sunday papers?

LORETTA: Life is sweet, Pachequín, and living it suits me fine.

PACHEQUIN: How can you possibly not fancy your picture in the Telegraph?

LORETTA: What a comedian!

PACHEQUIN: Does that mean you're not bowled over by the idea?

LORETTA: Right first time!

PACHEQUIN: That's hard to believe.

LORETTA: Just like your romancing.

PACHEQUIN: That's not a fair comparison. Tell me what I must do to prove my love, Loretta!

LORETTA: Nothing. Have some sense and stop upsetting me.

PACHEQUIN: Couldn't you love me just a little bit?

LORETTA: You've got up to a lot of no good in your time and you might well have to pay for it all at once.

PACHEQUIN: That would be fine by me as long as it was you dishing out the punishment.

LORETTA: You're forgetting about my husband.

PACHEQUIN: Give me your love then, for I've got a cape as good as Juan Belmonte's[1] to take care of that bull.

LORETTA: I can't love you, Pachequín.

PACHEQUIN: And can't you even give me the carnation you're wearing in your hair?

LORETTA: Why, doesn't it suit me?

PACHEQUIN: This lovely bloom in my lapel would suit you better. Shall we swap?

---

1   A bullfighter (1892-1962) renowned for his innovatory style. Note also the pun on "bull", a "horned" beast.

DOÑA LORETA: Como una fineza, Pachequín. Sin otra significación.
PACHEQUIN: Un día la rapto, Doña Loreta.
DOÑA LORETA: Peso mucho, Pachequín.
PACHEQUIN: ¡Levanto yo más quintales que San Cristóbal!
DOÑA LORETA: Con el pico.

Doña Loreta ríe, haciendo escalas buchonas, y se desprende el clavel del rodete. Las mangas del peinador escurren por los brazos desnudos de la Tenienta. En el silencio expresivo del cambio de miradas, una beata con manto de merinillo asoma por el atrio de Santiago: doña Tadea Calderón, que adusta y espantadiza, viendo el trueque de claveles, se santigua con la cruz del rosario. La tarasca, retirándose de la reja, toca hierro.

DOÑA LORETA: ¡Lagarto! ¡Lagarto! ¡Esa bruja me da espeluznos!

Doña Tadea pasa atisbando. El garabato de su silueta se recorta sobre el destello cegador y moruno de las casas encaladas. Se desvanece bajo un porche, y a poco, su cabeza de lechuza asoma en el ventano de una guardilla.

Escena tercera

El cementerio de Santiago el Verde: una tapia blanca con cipreses, y cancel negro con una cruz. Sobre la tierra removida, el capellán reza atropellado un responso, y el cortejo de mujerucas y marineros se dispersa. Al socaire de la tapia, como una sombra, va el teniente Don Friolera, que se cruza con algunos acompañantes del entierro. Juanito Pacheco, cojeando, pingona la capa, se le empareja.

PACHEQUIN: ¡Salud, mi Teniente!
DON FRIOLERA: Apártate, Pachequín.
PACHEQUIN: ¡Tiene usted la color mudada! ¡A usted le ocurre algún contratiempo!
DON FRIOLERA: No me interrogues.
PACHEQUIN: Manifiéstese usted con un amigo leal, mi Teniente.
DON FRIOLERA: Pachequín, ya llegará ocasión de que hablemos. Ahora sigue tu camino.
PACHEQUIN: Conforme, no quiero serle molesto, mi Teniente.
DON FRIOLERA: ¡Oye! ¿Por qué sales del cementerio?
PACHEQUIN: He venido dando convoy al cadáver de un parroquiano.
DON FRIOLERA: ¡Poca cosa! ...

LORETTA: As a token of esteem, Pachequín. Nothing more.
PACHEQUIN: One of these days I'll carry you off, Loretta.
LORETTA: I'd be a heavy burden, Pachequín.
PACHEQUIN: I can lift a bigger weight than Samson!
LORETTA: With your gob!

Loretta laughs, running up and down the scale of gut chuckles, and unfastens the carnation from her bun. The sleeves of the Lieutenant's Lady's dressing-gown slide up her bare arms. In the eloquent silence of their gaze, a sanctimonious old woman in a merino shawl appears in the church porch: Doña Tadea Calderón, who, on seeing the exchange of carnations, grimly and nervously blesses herself with the crucifix on her rosary. The floozie, stepping back from the grille, touches the iron bars for luck.

LORETTA: Watch out! Watch out! That old witch gives me the creeps!

Doña Tadea passes by, peeping inquisitively. Her pot-hook profile is silhouetted against the dazzling, Moorish gleam of the whitewashed houses. She disappears beneath an arcade and, shortly afterwards, her owl-like head appears at an attic window.

Scene Three

The graveyard of Santiago el Verde. A white wall with cypress trees and a wooden church-porch with a cross. Over the mound of dug-up earth, the chaplain leads a hasty responsory for the dead man, and the cortège of old biddies and sailors disperses. Along the shelter of the wall Lieutenant Mr Punch moves darkly by and passes some of those present at the funeral. Johnny Pacheco, in his shabby old cape, limps up to him.

PACHEQUIN: 'Afternoon, Lieutenant Sir.
MR PUNCH: Be off with you, Pachequín!
PACHEQUIN: You're as white as a sheet. Something untoward is troubling
          you.
MR PUNCH: Stop this interrogation now.
PACHEQUIN: Get it off you chest, Lieutenant. Tell a loyal friend all about it.
MR PUNCH: Pachequín, the time for us to speak will come sooner than you
          think. In the meantime, be about your business.
PACHEQUIN: As you wish, Lieutenant, I've no desire to bother you.
MR PUNCH: Wait! What are you doing coming out of the graveyard?
PACHEQUIN: I was here escorting the body of one of my customers.
MR PUNCH: Is that all!

PACHEQUIN: ¡Y tan poca!

DON FRIOLERA: No hablemos más. ¡Adiós!

PACHEQUIN: Todavía una palabra.

DON FRIOLERA: ¡Suéltala!

PACHEQUIN: ¿Qué le ocurre a usted, mi Teniente? ¡Abra usted su pecho a un
           amigo!

DON FRIOLERA: Verías el Infierno.

PACHEQUIN: ¡Le hallo a usted como estrafalario!

DON FRIOLERA: Estás en tu derecho.

*Don Friolera, haciendo gestos, se aleja pegado al blanco tapial de cipreses, y el
barbero, contoneándose con el ritmo desigual de la cojera, aborda un grupo de
tres sujetos marchosos que conversan en el campillo, frente a la negra cancela.
Aquel de la bufanda, calzones de odalisca y pedales amarillos, muy pinturero, es
el Niño del Melonar. Aquel pomposo pato azul con cresta roja, Curro Cadenas.
Y el que dogmatiza con el fagot bajo el carrik y el quepis sobre la oreja, Nelo el
Peneque.*

PACHEQUIN: ¡Salud, caballeros!

EL PENEQUE: ¡Salud, y pesetas!

PACHEQUIN: De eso hay poco.

EL PENEQUE: Pues son las mejores razones en este mundo.

CURRO: Esas ladronas nunca dejan de andar de por medio. Ellas y las mujeres
           son nuestra condenación.

EL NIÑO: ¿Tú qué dices, Pachequín?

PACHEQUIN: Aprendo la doctrina.

EL NIÑO: Cultivando a la Tenienta.

CURRO: ¡No es mala mujer!

EL PENEQUE: Cartagenera y esposa de militar, pues dicho se está que buen
           pico, buen garbo y buena pierna.

PACHEQUIN: En ese respecto, un servidor se declara incompetente.

EL NIÑO: ¿Todavía no le has regalado unas ligas a la Tenienta?

PACHEQUIN: Caballeros, con tanta risa van ustedes a sentir disnea.

EL PENEQUE: No te ofendas, ninche.

PACHEQUIN: Doña Loreta es una esposa fiel a sus deberes. La amistad que me
           une con su esposo es la filarmonía. Don Pascual es un fenómeno
           de los buenos haciendo sonar la guitarra.

PACHEQUIN: Sure enough.

MR PUNCH: There's nothing more to be said then. Good-bye.

PACHEQUIN: Just a little word in your ear.

MR PUNCH: Go on then.

PACHEQUIN: What's the matter with you, Lieutenant? Open your heart up to a
friend.

MR PUNCH: You'd see Hell itself.

PACHEQUIN: You seem to be acting very peculiar.

MR PUNCH: You're perfectly entitled to your own opinion.

*Mr Punch, gesticulating the while, moves away, skirting the white wall by the
cypresses, and the barber, swaggering with the uneven rhythm of his lameness,
approaches a trio of wide-boys in conversation in the small field opposite the
black church-porch. The one wearing a scarf, odalisque breeches and yellow spats
is the swanky Cantaloupe Kid; the pompous, red-crested blue duck is Flash
Frank Cadenas and the one laying down the law, with his military cap over one
ear and a bassoon under his gabardine, is Manny the Jug-head.*

PACHEQUIN: God rest you, gentlemen.

JUG-HEAD: God rest us and send us a few bob.

PACHEQUIN: You don't see many of them about these days.

JUG-HEAD: That's true, but they're what makes the world go round.

FLASH FRANK: Those little beauties are forever catching your eye. It's
women and them that'll be the death of us all.

THE KID: What have you got to say about that, Pachequín?

PACHEQUIN: I'm just a student at that university.

THE KID: Chatting up the Lieutenant's Lady.

FLASH FRANK: She's a fine figure of a woman!

JUG-HEAD: From Cartagena,[1] and you know what they say about soldiers'
wives. I've heard she has a cute little beak, bags of style and is
more than a bit tidy in the leg region.

PACHEQUIN: In that region yours truly is not qualified to comment.

THE KID: Have you still not presented the Lieutenant's Lady with a pair of
garters?

PACHEQUIN: Gentlemen, if you carry on laughing so much, you're liable to
choke.

JUG-HEAD: Don't get upset, sunbeam.

PACHEQUIN: Loretta is a faithful and a dutiful wife. The friendship which
conjoins her husband and myself is totally philharmonic. Pascual
is no slouch where there's a nifty bit of fiddling[2] to be done.

---

1 Cartagena is an important port and military base on the south-east coast of Spain.

2 Guitar-playing is, in the original, a metaphor for illicit dealing. For that reason it
has been rendered into English as 'fiddling'.

EL PENEQUE: ¡La mejor guitarra está hoy en el Presidio de Cartagena!

EL NIÑO: ¿A quién señalas?

EL PENEQUE: Al Pollo de Triana.

PACHEQUIN: Don Pascual tiene un estilo parejo.

EL PENEQUE: No le conocía yo esa gracia.

PACHEQUIN: ¡Un coloso!

CURRO: No miente el amigo. A Don Friolera vengo yo tratándole hace muchos años. En la Plaza de Algeciras le he conocido sirviendo en clase de sargento, y tuve ocasión de oírle algunos conciertos. ¡Es una guitarra de las buenas! Entonces Don Friolera estaba tenido por sujeto mirado y servicial, de lo mas razonable y decente del Cuerpo de Carabineros.

EL NIÑO: ¡Menudo cambiazo el que ha dado! Hoy pone la cucaña en el Pico de Teide.[1]

EL PENEQUE: Pues la mucha familia no le obliga a ese rigor.

EL NIÑO: Es la obra de los galones. Se ha desvanecido. En una pacotilla de cien duros, a lo presente, te pide un quiñón de veinticinco.

PACHEQUIN: Hoy los duros son pesetas. No están las cosas como hace algunos años.

EL PENEQUE: ¡Y todo este desavío nos lo trajo el Kaiser!

CURRO: ¡Y aun ha de tardar el arreglo! La España de cabo a cabo hemos de verla como está Barcelona. Y el que honradamente juntó cuatro cuartos, tendrá que suicidarse.

Se alejan haciendo estaciones. Sobre las cuatro figuras en hilera ondula una ráfaga de viento. Anochece. El Teniente, con gestos de maníaco, viene bordeando la tapia, pasa bajo la sombra de los cipreses, y continúa la ronda del cementerio. Bultos negros de mujerucas con rebozos salpican el campillo. El Teniente se cruza con una vieja que le clava los ojos de pajarraco: pequeña, cetrina, ratonil, va cubierta con un manto de merinillo. Don Friolera siente el peso de aquella mirada y una súbita iluminación. Se vuelve y atrapa a la beata por el moño.

DON FRIOLERA: ¡Doña Tadea, merece usted morir quemada!

DOÑA TADEA: ¡Está usted loco!

DON FRIOLERA: ¡Quemada por bruja!

---

1   Situated in the Canary Islands, the Pico de Teide is the highest mountain in Spain.

JUG-HEAD: The finest fiddler around is now in the clink in Cartagena!

THE KID: To whom do you refer?

JUG-HEAD: The Triana Trotter.

PACHEQUIN: Pascual has a similar style.

JUG-HEAD: I wasn't aware of his talent in that area.

PACHEQUIN: Quite outstanding.

FLASH FRANK: It's no lie that our friend here is telling. I've had dealings with Mr Punch over a number of years. I first came across him at H.Q. in Algeciras when he was a sergeant and had occasion to hear some of of his scratching. One of the finest fiddlers in the business. In those days Mr Punch was very highly thought of and considered most accommodating; the most reasonable and decent sort in the whole corps.

THE KID: Then it's a change and a half that's come over him! His prices have gone through the roof these days.

JUG-HEAD: It's hardly as if he's got a large family to support.

THE KID: It's the pips that are to blame. He's lost all touch. At the moment for every hundred-bob haul he asks you for a cut of twenty-five.

PACHEQUIN: A bob these days is hardly worth a penny. Things ain't what they used to be!

JUG-HEAD: The Kaiser's[1] to blame for all this nonsense.

FLASH FRANK: And it's going to be a while before it all gets sorted out. In no time the whole of Spain will be just like Barcelona[2] is now. And your poor sod who's scraped a couple of honest bob together might as well go and top himself.

They walk haltingly off. A gust of wind ripples over the four figures in line. Night is falling. The Lieutenant, gesticulating like a maniac, skirts the wall, passes under the shade of the cypress-trees and continues circling the graveyard. Black shapes of muffled old women speckle the small field. The Lieutenant comes across one of them, who fixes her hawkish old eyes upon him. Tiny, jaundiced and mouse-like, she has a merino shawl draped over her. Mr Punch feels the weight of her gaze and is struck by a sudden insight. He spins around and grabs the woman by her hair-piece.

MR PUNCH: Doña Tadea, you ought to be burned at the stake!

DOÑA TADEA: You're round the twist!

MR PUNCH: Burned as a witch!

---

1 Spain's neutrality in the Great War led eventually to inflationary pressures, as well as creating considerable friction between the supporters of the Allies and those of the Germanic Powers.

2 The contemporary situation in Barcelona was one of open street-warfare between revolutionary workers on one side and the employers and authorities on the other.

DOÑA TADEA: ¡No me falte usted!

DON FRIOLERA: ¡Usted ha escrito el anónimo!

DOÑA TADEA: ¡Respete usted que soy una anciana!

DON FRIOLERA: ¡Usted lo ha escrito!

DOÑA TADEA: ¡Mentira!

DON FRIOLERA: ¿Sabe usted a lo que me refiero?

DOÑA TADEA: No sé nada, ni me importa.

DON FRIOLERA: Va usted a escupir esa lengua de serpiente. ¡Usted me ha robado el sosiego!

DOÑA TADEA: Piense usted si otros no le robaron algo más.

DON FRIOLERA: ¡Perra!

DOÑA TADEA: ¡Suélteme usted! ¡Ay! ¡Ay!

DON FRIOLERA: ¡Bruja! ¡Me ha mordido la mano!

DOÑA TADEA: ¡Asesino! Devuélvame el postizo del moño.

DON FRIOLERA: ¡Arpía! ¿Por qué ha escrito esa infamia?

DOÑA TADEA: ¡Se atreve usted con una pobre vieja, y con quien debe atreverse, mucha ceremonia!

DON FRIOLERA: ¡Mujer infernal!

DOÑA TADEA: ¡Grosero!

DON FRIOLERA: ¡Usted ha escrito el papel!

DOÑA TADEA: ¡Chiflado!

DON FRIOLERA: ¡Pero usted sabe que soy un cabrón!

DOÑA TADEA: Lo sabe el pueblo entero. ¡Suélteme usted! Debe usted sangrarse.

DON FRIOLERA: ¡Aborto infernal!

DOÑA TADEA: ¡Me da usted lástima!

DON FRIOLERA: ¿Con quién me la pega mi mujer?

DOÑA TADEA: Eso le incumbe a usted averiguarlo. Vigile usted.

DON FRIOLERA: ¿Y para qué, si no puedo volver a ser feliz?

DOÑA TADEA: Tiene usted una hija, edúquela usted, sin malos ejemplos. Viva usted para ella.

DON FRIOLERA: ¿El ladrón de mi honra, es Pachequín?

DOÑA TADEA: ¿A qué pregunta, Señor Teniente? Usted puede sorprender el adulterio, si disimula y anda alertado.

DON FRIOLERA: ¿Y para qué?

DOÑA TADEA: Para dar a los culpables su merecido.

DON FRIOLERA: ¡La muerte!

DOÑA TADEA: ¡Virgen Santa!

La vieja gazmoña huye enseñando las canillas. Don Friolera se sienta al pie del negro cancel, y dando un suspiro, a media voz, inicia su monólogo de cornudo.

DOÑA TADEA: How dare you!

MR PUNCH: It was you sent me the tip-off!

DOÑA TADEA: Show some respect for a poor old woman!

MR PUNCH: You were the one that wrote it!

DOÑA TADEA: That's a lie!

MR PUNCH: Do you know what I'm talking about?

DOÑA TADEA: I haven't got a clue and I couldn't care less.

MR PUNCH: You're going to spit out that serpent's tongue of yours. You've
robbed me of my peace of mind!

DOÑA TADEA: Well, just think about whether someone else hasn't robbed you
of a lot more.

MR PUNCH: You bitch!

DOÑA TADEA: You're hurting me, ouch!

MR PUNCH: You rotten old hag, you've bitten my hand!

DOÑA TADEA: You murderer, give me back my hair-piece!

MR PUNCH: Why did you write such infamy, you harpy?

DOÑA TADEA: Go on, attack a poor old woman, then, but as for the guilty
party there's nothing but sweetness and light!

MR PUNCH: Infernal woman!

DOÑA TADEA: Don't be so uncouth!

MR PUNCH: It was you who wrote the note!

DOÑA TADEA: You're off your rocker!

MR PUNCH: But you know that I'm a cuckold!

DOÑA TADEA: The whole town knows it. Let go of me! You need to see a
doctor.

MR PUNCH: You abomination!

DOÑA TADEA: You make me want to cry!

MR PUNCH: Who's knocking a slice off my missus?

DOÑA TADEA: That's up to you to find out. Keep your eyes open.

MR PUNCH: What's the point if I can never be happy again?

DOÑA TADEA: You've got your little girl. Bring her up decent. Keep her away
from bad examples. Live just for her.

MR PUNCH: The thief of my honour, it's Pachequín, isn't it?

DOÑA TADEA: Why ask me, Lieutenant? You can catch them in the act if you
don't let on and keep your eyes open.

MR PUNCH: What for?

DOÑA TADEA: To give the sinners their just deserts.

MR PUNCH: Kill them!

DOÑA TADEA: Holy Mother of God!

*The old hypocrite rushes off showing her shanks. Mr Punch sits at the bottom
of the black porch and, with a sigh and half under his breath, begins his
cuckold's monologue.*

Escena cuarta

La costanilla de Santiago el Verde, cuando las estrellas hacen guiños sobre los tejados. Un borracho sale bailando a la puerta del billar de doña Calixta. La última beata vuelve de la novena. Arrebujada en su manto de merinillo, pasa fisgona metiendo el hocico por rejas y puertas. En el claro de luna, el garabato de su sombra tiene reminiscencias de vulpeja. Escurridiza, desaparece bajo los porches y reaparece sobre la banda de luz que vierte la reja de una sala baja y domínguera, alumbrada por quinqué de porcelana azul. Se detiene a espiar. Don Friolera, sentado ante el velador con tapete de malla, sostiene abierto un álbum de retratos. Se percibe el pueril y cristalino punteado de su caja de música. Don Friolera, en el reflejo amarillo del quinqué, es un fantoche trágico. La beata se acerca, y pega a la reja su perfil de lechuza. El Teniente levanta la cabeza, y los dos se miran un instante.

DOÑA TADEA: ¡Esta tarde me ha dado usted un susto! Podía haberle denunciado.

DON FRIOLERA: ¡Antes había recibido una puñalada en el corazon!

DOÑA TADEA: ¡Es usted maniático, Señor Teniente!

DON FRIOLERA: Doña Tadea, usted está siempre como una lechuza en la ventana de su guardilla, usted sabe quién entra y sale en cada casa ... ¡Doña Tadea maldita, usted ha escrito el anónimo!

DOÑA TADEA: ¡Jesús María!

DON FRIOLERA: ¡Aun conserva la tinta en las uñas!

DOÑA TADEA: ¡Falsario!

DON FRIOLERA: ¿Por qué ha encendido usted esta hoguera en mi alma?

DOÑA TADEA: ¡Calumniador!

DON FRIOLERA: ¡Sólo usted conocía mi deshonra!

DOÑA TADEA: ¡Papanatas!

DON FRIOLERA: ¡Doña Tadea, merecía usted ser quemada!

DOÑA TADEA: ¡Y usted llevar la corona que lleva!

DON FRIOLERA: Yo soy militar y haré un disparate.

DOÑA TADEA: ¡Ave María! ¡Por culpa de dos réprobos una tragedia en nuestra calle!

DON FRIOLERA: ¡Considere usted el caso!

DOÑA TADEA: ¡Porque lo considero, Señor Teniente!

DON FRIOLERA: ¡El honor se lava con sangre!

DOÑA TADEA: ¡Eso decían antaño! ...

DON FRIOLERA: ¡Cuando quemaban a las brujas!

Scene Four

The steep street leading up to Santiago el Verde, the stars winking above the roof-tops. A drunk staggers out of the door of Calixta's billiard saloon. The last devout old woman is returning home after her novena. Wrapped tightly in her merino shawl, she sniffs around, poking her snout into doorways and window-grilles. In the clear moonlight her pot-hook shadow has something vixen-like about it. Scurrying, she disappears beneath the arcade and reappears in the swathe of light spilling out of the window-grille of a downstairs parlour, illuminated by a blue porcelain oil-lamp. She stops to spy. Mr Punch, sitting at a pedestal table with a crochet cover, is holding open a photograph album. The tinkling and childish notes of his musical box can be heard. Mr Punch, in the yellow light of the oil-lamp, is a tragic puppet. The sanctimonious old woman steps closer and presses her owlish face to the grille. The Lieutenant raises his head and they hold each other's gaze for a moment.

DOÑA TADEA: You gave me a real fright this evening! I could have had you arrested.

MR PUNCH: You'd have got a knife in your heart if you'd tried!

DOÑA TADEA: You're demented, Lieutenant!

MR PUNCH: Doña Tadea, you're always perched up there like an owl in your attic window, you see all the comings and goings ... Damn you, Doña Tadea, it was you that wrote the tip-off!

DOÑA TADEA: Heaven preserve us!

MR PUNCH: You've still got the ink on your fingernails!

DOÑA TADEA: Liar!

MR PUNCH: What made you light this blaze in my heart?

DOÑA TADEA: Slanderer!

MR PUNCH: No-one but you knew my honour was lost!

DOÑA TADEA: Stupid twit!

MR PUNCH: Doña Tadea, you deserve to be burned at the stake.

DOÑA TADEA: And you deserve to be the cuckold you are.

MR PUNCH: I'm an army officer, I'll do something desperate.

DOÑA TADEA: Holy Mother of God! A tragedy in our street because of two wicked sinners!

MR PUNCH: Just think what it means!

DOÑA TADEA: That's just what I am doing, Lieutenant!

MR PUNCH: A man's honour can only be washed clean with blood!

DOÑA TADEA: So they said in the good old days! ...

MR PUNCH: When they burned witches at the stake!

DOÑA TADEA: ¡Señor Teniente, no tenga usted para mí tan negra entraña! ...
         Pudiera ser que no hubiese fornicio. Usted, guarde a su esposa.
DON FRIOLERA: ¿Quién ha escrito el anónimo, Doña Tadea?
DOÑA TADEA: ¡Yo sólo sé mis pecados!

La vieja se arrebuja en el manto, desaparece en la sombra de la callejuela, reaparece en el ventano de su guardilla, y bajo la luna, espía con ojos de lechuza. Santiguándose oye el cisma de los malcasados. Don Friolera y Doña Loreta riñen a gritos, baten las puertas, entran y salen con los brazos abiertos. Sobre el velador con tapete de malla, el quinqué de porcelana azul alumbra la sala dominguera. El movimiento de las figuras, aquel entrar y salir con los brazos abiertos, tienen la sugestión de una tragedia de fantoches.

DON FRIOLERA: ¡Es inaudito!
DOÑA LORETA: ¡Palabrotas, no!
DON FRIOLERA: ¡Dejarte cortejar!
DOÑA LORETA: ¡Una fineza no es un cortejo!
DON FRIOLERA: ¡Has abierto un abismo entre nosotros! ¡Un abismo de los
         llamados insondables!
DOÑA LORETA: ¡Farolón!
DON FRIOLERA: ¡Estás buscando que te mate, Loreta! ¡Que lave mi honor
         con tu sangre!
DOÑA LORETA: ¡Hazlo! ¡Solamente por verte subir al patíbulo lo estoy
         deseando!
DON FRIOLERA: ¡Disipada!
DOÑA LORETA: ¡Verdugo!

Don Friolera blande un pistolón. Doña Loreta, con los brazos en aspa y el moño colgando, sale de la casa dando gritos. Don Friolera la persigue, y en el umbral de la puerta, al pisar la calle, la sujeta por los pelos.

DON FRIOLERA: ¡Vas a morir!
DOÑA LORETA: ¡Asesino!
DON FRIOLERA: ¡Encomiéndate a Dios!
DOÑA LORETA: ¡Criminal! ¡Que con las armas de fuego no hay bromas!

Ábrese repentinamente la ventana del barbero, y éste asoma en jubón de franela amarilla, el pescuezo todo nuez.

PACHEQUIN: ¿Va el pueblo a consentir este mal trato? Si otro no se
         interpone, yo me interpongo, porque la mata.

DOÑA TADEA: Lieutenant, there's no call for such hatred in your heart towards
me!... No actual fornication may have occurred. You just take
good care of your wife.

MR PUNCH: Who wrote the tip-off, Doña Tadea?

DOÑA TADEA: I only know my own sins!

*The old woman wraps her shawl more tightly around herself and disappears into
the shadows of the narrow street, only to reappear at her attic window, where she
keeps watch in the moonlight with her owl's eyes. She blesses herself as she
listens to the unhappy marriage breaking up. Mr Punch and Loretta are having a
screaming row, slamming doors and running in and out with their arms flung
wide. On the table with the crochet cover, the blue porcelain oil-lamp lights up
the parlour. The way the figures move, the entrances and exits with arms flung
out, all give the impression of a tragic puppet-show.*

MR PUNCH: I'm absolutely flabbergasted!

LORETTA: Mind your language!

MR PUNCH: Letting yourself be chatted up!

LORETTA: A token of esteem isn't being chatted up!

MR PUNCH: You've opened an abyss between us! What they call a fathomless
abyss!

LORETTA: Swallowed a dictionary, have we?

MR PUNCH: You'll force me to kill you, Loretta, to cleanse the stain on my
honour with your blood!

LORETTA: Go on then, do it! It'll be worth it, just to see you hanged!

MR PUNCH: Hussy!

LORETTA: Butcher!

*Mr Punch brandishes a blunderbuss. Loretta, her arms flung wide, her hair-bun
hanging in disarray, runs out of the house shrieking. Mr Punch chases her and
grabs her by the hair just as she reaches the street outside the door.*

MR PUNCH: You're going to die!

LORETTA: Murderer!

MR PUNCH: Commend your soul to God!

LORETTA: You great thug! You don't mess around with loaded guns!

*The window of the barber's house suddenly opens and he looks out, wearing a
yellow flannel vest, his scrawny throat all Adam's apple.*

PACHEQUIN: Aren't the townsfolk going to stop this violence? I'll intervene,
even if no-one else will, otherwise he'll kill her.

Empuñando un estoque de bastón, salta a la calle, y con su zanco desigual se
dirige a la casa de la tragedia.

DON FRIOLERA: ¡Traidor! Te alojaré una bala en la cabeza.

PACHEQUIN: ¡Verdugo de su señora, que no se la merece!

DON FRIOLERA: ¡Ladrón de mi honor!

PACHEQUIN: ¡A las mujeres se las respeta!

DON FRIOLERA: ¡No admito lecciones!

DOÑA LORETA: ¡Pascualín!

DON FRIOLERA: ¡Pascual! ¡Para la esposa adúltera, Pascual!

DOÑA LORETA: ¡No te ofusques!

DON FRIOLERA: ¡Os mataré a los dos!

DOÑA LORETA: ¡No des una campanada, Pascual!

DON FRIOLERA: ¡Pido cuentas de mi honor!

DOÑA LORETA: ¡Pascualín!

DON FRIOLERA: ¡Exijo que me llames Pascual!

PACHEQUIN: ¡No lleva usted razón, mi Teniente!

DON FRIOLERA: ¡Falso amigo, esa mujer debiera ser sagrada para ti!

PACHEQUIN: ¡Así la he considerado siempre!

DON FRIOLERA: ¿Loreta, quién te dio esa flor que llevas en el rodete?

DOÑA LORETA: Una fineza.

PACHEQUIN: No vea usted en ello mala intención, mi Teniente.

DOÑA LORETA: ¡Pascualín!

DON FRIOLERA: ¡Pascual! ¡Para ti ya no soy Pascualín!

DOÑA LORETA: ¡Rechazas un mimo, ya no me quieres!

DON FRIOLERA: ¡No puedo quererte!

PACHEQUIN: Perdone que se lo diga, pero no merece usted la perla que tiene,
          mi Teniente.

DON FRIOLERA: Con vuestra sangre lavaré mi honra. Vais a morir los dos.

PACHEQUIN: Mi Teniente, oiga razones.

DOÑA LORETA: ¡Ciego! ¿No ves resplandecer nuestra inocencia?

DON FRIOLERA: ¡Encomiéndense ustedes a Dios!

PACHEQUIN: ¿Doña Loreta, qué hacemos?

DOÑA LORETA: ¡Rezar, Pachequín!

PACHEQUIN: ¿Vamos a dejar que nos mate como perros? ¡Doña Loreta, no
          puede ser!

DOÑA LORETA: ¡Pachequín, tenga usted esta flor, culpa de los celos de mi
          esposo!

Grasping his sword-stick, he jumps out into the street and with his dot-and-carry gait moves toward the house of tragedy.

MR PUNCH: You double-crosser! I'm going to blow your brains out.

PACHEQUIN: Wife-killer! She's too good for you!

MR PUNCH: You've filched my honour, you thief!

PACHEQUIN: Women should be treated with respect!

MR PUNCH: Don't you lecture me!

LORETTA: Paskie!

MR PUNCH: Pascual! My name is Pascual, you adulteress!

LORETTA: Try to understand!

MR PUNCH: I'll kill the pair of you!

LORETTA: Don't make a scene, Pascual!

MR PUNCH: I demand satisfaction for my honour!

LORETTA: Paskie!

MR PUNCH: I insist you call me Pascual!

PACHEQUIN: You're making a mistake, Lieutenant Sir!

MR PUNCH: You cheat! So-called friend, this woman should have been sacred in your eyes!

PACHEQUIN: So has she always been!

MR PUNCH: Loretta, who gave you that flower you're wearing in your hair?

LORETTA: It was just an innocent gift, that's all.

PACHEQUIN: Don't think for a moment there was anything else in it, Lieutenant Sir.

LORETTA: Paskie!

MR PUNCH: Pascual! I'm not your Paskie any more!

LORETTA: You won't let me cuddle you, you don't love me!

MR PUNCH: I can't love you!

PACHEQUIN: Forgive my saying so, Lieutenant Sir, but you don't deserve the jewel of a wife you've got.

MR PUNCH: I'll wash my honour clean in your blood. You're both going to die.

PACHEQUIN: Lieutenant Sir, listen to reason.

LORETTA: You must be blind! Our innocence is as clear as daylight.

MR PUNCH: Make your peace with God!

PACHEQUIN: Loretta, what shall we do?

LORETTA: Pray, Pachequín!

PACHEQUIN: Are we going to let him shoot us down like dogs? That can't be right, Loretta!

LORETTA: Pachequín, take back this flower, the cause of my husband's jealousy!

Doña Loreta, con ademán trágico, se desprende el clavel que baila al extremo del moño colgante. Pachequín alarga la mano. Don Friolera se interpone, arrebata la flor y la pisotea. La tarasca cae de rodillas, abre los brazos y ofrece el pecho a las furias del pistolón.

DOÑA LORETA: ¡Mátame! ¡Moriré inocente!
DON FRIOLERA: ¡Morirás cuando yo lo ordene!

Una niña, como moña de feria, descalza, en camisa, con el pelo suelto, aparece dando gritos en la reja.

LA NIÑA: ¡Papito! ¡Papín!
DOÑA LORETA: ¡Hija mía, acabas de perder a tu madre!

Don Friolera arroja el pistolón, se oprime las sienes, y arrebatado entra en la casa, cerrando la puerta. Se le ve aparecer en la reja, tomar en brazos a la niña y besarla llorando, ridículo y viejo.

DON FRIOLERA: ¡Manolita, pon un bálsamo en el corazón de tu papá!

Doña Loreta, caída sobre las rodillas, golpea la puerta, grita sofocada, se araña y se mesa.

DOÑA LORETA: ¡Pascual, mira lo que haces! ¡Limpia estoy de toda culpa! ¡En adelante, quizá no pueda decirlo, pues me abandonas, y la mujer abandonada, santa ha de ser para no escuchar al Diablo! ¡Ábreme la puerta, mal hombre! ... ¡Dame tu ayuda, Reina y Madre!

La tarasca bate con la frente en la puerta y se desmaya. Pachequín mira de reojo al fondo de la sala silenciosa, y acude a tenerla. La tarasca suspira transportada.

DOÑA LORETA: ¡Peso mucho!
PACHEQUIN: ¡No importa! Mientras no pasa este nublado, acepte usted el abrigo de mis tejas.

Se abren algunas ventanas, y asoman en retablo figuras en camisa, con un gesto escandalizado. Pachequín se vuelve y hace un corte de mangas.

Loretta, with a tragic gesture, unfastens the carnation which is bobbing on the end of her dangling hair-bun. Pachequín stretches out his hand. Mr Punch jumps between them, snatches the flower and stamps on it. The floozie falls to her knees, opens her arms wide and offers her bosom to the fury of the blunderbuss.

LORETTA: Kill me then! I die innocent!
MR PUNCH: You die when I say so!

A little girl, pretty as a fairground doll, barefoot in her nightie, her hair loose, appears at the window-grille and calls out.

LITTLE GIRL: Daddy! Daddy!
LORETTA: My darling child! You'll never see your mother again!

Mr Punch hurls the blunderbuss from him, clasps his head in his hands and runs into the house, shutting the door. He reappears at the window-grille, and can be seen taking the little girl in his arms and kissing her; he looks old and ridiculous as he weeps.

MR PUNCH: My little Manolita, soothe your daddy's aching heart!

Loretta, on her knees, bangs at the door, crying out, rending her clothes and tearing her hair.

LORETTA: Pascual, think what you're doing! I'm not guilty of anything! I
          might not be able to say the same after this, because you've cast
          me out, and an abandoned wife needs to be a saint not to fall into
          temptation! Open the door, you wicked man! ... Holy Mother of
          God, help me!

The floozie beats her head against the door and sinks to the ground. Pachequín darts a sideways glance at the now empty room and comes to hold her. The floozie sighs rapturously.

LORETTA: I'm a heavy burden!
PACHEQUIN: No matter! I offer you shelter under my roof until this thunder-
          cloud passes.

Windows open and there appears a puppet-show of figures in nightshirts striking scandalised postures. Pachequín turns round and gives them two fingers.

PACHEQUIN: ¡El mundo me la da, pues yo la tomo, como dice el eminente
           Echegaray!
DOÑA TADEA: ¡Piedra de escándalo!

Escena quinta

La alcoba del barbero. Pegada a la pared, la cama angosta y hopada, con una colcha vistosa de pájaros y ramajes, un paraíso portugués. Tras de la puerta, la capa y la gorra colgadas con la guitarra, fingen un bulto viviente. Por el ventano abierto penetra, con el claro de luna, el ventalle silencioso y nocturno de un huerto de luceros. Y la brisa y la luna parecen conducir un diálogo entre el vestiglo de la puerta y el pelele, que abre la cruz de los brazos sobre la copa negra de una higuera, en la redoma azul del huerto. Entra el galán con la raptada, encendida, pomposa y con suspiros de soponcio. La luna infla los carrillos en la ventana.

DOÑA LORETA: ¿Demonio tentador, adónde me conduces?
PACHEQUIN: ¡A tu casa, prenda!
DOÑA LORETA: ¡Buscas la perdición de los dos! ¡Tú eres un falso! ¡Déjame
           volver honrada al lado de mi esposo! ¡Demonio tentador, no te
           interpongas!
PACHEQUIN: ¿Ya no soy nada para ti, mujer fatal? ¿Ya no dicto ninguna
           palabra a tu corazón? ¡Juntos hemos arrostrado la sentencia de ese
           hombre bárbaro que no te merece!
DOÑA LORETA: Yo lo elegí libremente.
PACHEQUIN: ¡Estabas ofuscada!
DOÑA LORETA: ¿Y ahora no es ofuscación dejar mi casa, dejar un ser nacido
           de mis entrañas? ¡Considera que soy esposa y madre!
PACHEQUIN: ¡Todo lo considero! ... ¡Y también que tu vida peligra al lado de
           ese hombre celoso!
DOÑA LORETA: ¡No me ciegues y ábreme la puerta!
PACHEQUIN: ¿Olvidas que una misma bala pudo matarnos?
DOÑA LORETA: ¡No me ciegues! ¡Ten un buen proceder, y ábreme la puerta!

PACHEQUIN: They all claim I've had her, so I might as well take her, as the
    distinguished Echegaray[1] says in his play!
DOÑA TADEA: What a scandal!

Scene Five

*The barber's bedroom. Tight up against the wall, a narrow billowed bed with a
colourful counterpane of birds and branches – a Portuguese paradise. Behind the
door, the cape and cap draped over the guitar have the shape of a living body.
Through the open window there enters, with the moonlight, the silent nocturnal
waft of a starry orchard. The breeze and the moon seem to conduct a dialogue
between the monster on the door and the scarecrow-like figure waving his arms
in the blackness at the top of the fig-tree in the blue bulbous bell-jar of the
orchard. The gallant enters with his prize, who is flushed and majestic in a
sighing swoon. The moon swells her cheeks in the window.*

LORETTA: Whither do you take me, you silver-tongued rogue?
PACHEQUIN: To your home, my sweet.
LORETTA: You'll be the ruination of us both! You're not to be trusted! Let me
    return to my husband with my virtue intact! Don't come between
    us, you sweet-talking devil!
PACHEQUIN: Do I mean so little to you now, you scarlet woman? Have I no
    words to touch your heart? Together we've defied the rage of that
    barbarian who's unworthy of you!
LORETTA: I chose him of my own free will.
PACHEQUIN: Ah, but you were bedazzled!
LORETTA: And is this now no bedazzlement, to leave my home, to leave the
    flesh of my flesh? Have some consideration. I am a wife and
    mother!
PACHEQUIN: I take everything into consideration! ... Especially that your life
    is in peril at the hands of that jealous man!
LORETTA: Release me from your spell and open the door!
PACHEQUIN: Do you forget that both of us could have perished by a single
    shot?
LORETTA: You're making my head spin! Be a decent fellow and open the door!

---

1 A pillar of the establishment, and a highly successful engineer and politician as
   well as a fashionable dramatist, José Echegaray (1833-1916) was the frequent
   butt of Valle's witticisms. Parodied here are the closing lines of his *El gran
   galeoto (The Great Go-Between)*, a melodrama of 1881 portraying a platonic
   friendship between a young man and a married woman which results in the death
   of the husband in a duel instigated by malicious gossip.

PACHEQUIN: ¿Olvidas que nuestra sangre estuvo a pique de correr emparejada?

DOÑA LORETA: ¡No me ciegues!

PACHEQUIN: ¿Olvidas que ese hombre bárbaro, a los dos nos tuvo encañonados con su pistola? ¿Qué mayor lazo para enlazar corazones?

DOÑA LORETA: ¡No pretendo romperlo! ¡Pero déjame volver al lado de mi hija, que estoy en el mundo para mirar por ella!

PACHEQUIN: ¿Y para nada más?

DOÑA LORETA: ¡Y para quererte, demonio tentador!

PACHEQUIN: ¿Por qué entonces huyes de mi lado?

DOÑA LORETA: ¡Porque me das miedo!

PACHEQUIN: ¡No paso a creerlo! ¡Tú buscas verme desesperado!

DOÑA LORETA: ¡Calla, traidor!

PACHEQUIN: Si me amases, estarías recogida en mis brazos, como una paloma.

DOÑA LORETA: ¿Por qué así me hablas, cuando sabes que soy tuya?

PACHEQUIN: ¡Aun no lo has sido!

DOÑA LORETA: Lo seré y te cansarás de tenerme, pero ahora no me pidas cosa ninguna.

PACHEQUIN: Me pondré de rodillas.

DOÑA LORETA: ¡Pachequín, respétame! ¡Yo soy una romántica!

PACHEQUIN: En ese achaque no me superas. Cuando te contemplo, amor mío, me entra como éxtasis.

DOÑA LORETA: ¡Qué noche de luceros!

PACHEQUIN: ¡La propia para un idilio!

DOÑA LORETA: ¡Dame una prueba de amor puro!

PACHEQUIN: ¡La que me pidas!

DOÑA LORETA: ¡Permite que me vaya! ¡Ten un noble proceder y ábreme la puerta!

PACHEQUIN: ¡Franca la tienes!

DOÑA LORETA: ¡Adiós, Juanito!

PACHEQUIN: ¡Adiós, Loreta!

DOÑA LORETA: ¿No quiere usted mirarme?

PACHEQUIN: ¡No puedo! ¡Temo perder el juicio y olvidarme de que soy un caballero! ¡Ahí son nada tus miradas, Loreta!

DOÑA LORETA: ¡Es de rosas y espinas nuestra cadena!

PACHEQUIN: ¡Tú la rompes!

DOÑA LORETA: ¡No me ciegues!

PACHEQUIN: ¿Adónde vas? ¡Cortemos, Loreta, ese nudo gordiano!

PACHEQUIN: Do you forget how close our blood came to mingling in the same stream?

LORETTA: Don't bedazzle me!

PACHEQUIN: Do you forget how that barbarian had both of us in the sights of his gun? What better knot is there to bind our hearts together?

LORETTA: I do not seek to break it! But let me return to my daughter's side. My duty in this world is but to care for her!

PACHEQUIN: And for nothing else?

LORETTA: And to love you too, you silver-tongued devil!

PACHEQUIN: Why, then, do you flee from my embrace?

LORETTA: Because I'm afraid of you!

PACHEQUIN: How can I believe it? You seek merely to plunge me into despair!

LORETTA: No more, you wicked seducer!

PACHEQUIN: If you loved me, you'd nestle in my arms like a dove.

LORETTA: Why do you speak to me in this way when you know I'm yours?

PACHEQUIN: I haven't had you yet!

LORETTA: You will, and you'll have your fill of me; but for the moment, ask no more.

PACHEQUIN: I'll get down on my knees.

LORETTA: Have some regard for me, Pachequín, I'm a romantic!

PACHEQUIN: I'm of the same persuasion myself. My love, when I gaze upon you I come over all ecstatic.

LORETTA: What a lovely starry night!

PACHEQUIN: Made to measure for an idyll!

LORETTA: Give me some proof of the pureness of your love!

PACHEQUIN: Ask anything of me!

LORETTA: Let me go! Make a noble gesture and open the door!

PACHEQUIN: For you it stands unbolted!

LORETTA: Farewell, my Johnny!

PACHEQUIN: Adieu, Loretta mine!

LORETTA: Won't you even look at me?

PACHEQUIN: I can't! I'm afraid I'll lose my head and forget I'm a gentleman! You don't know what you do to me, Loretta!

LORETTA: Of roses and thorns is our chain made!

PACHEQUIN: And you contrive to sever it!

LORETTA: Don't bedazzle me!

PACHEQUIN: Whither are you going? Let us cut, Loretta, this Gordian knot.[1]

---

1 An allusion to Eugenio Selles' melodrama of the same name, published in 1868, in which the aggrieved husband kills his wife as she prepares to elope with her lover.

DOÑA LORETA: ¡Soy esposa y madre!

PACHEQUIN: Temo que te asesine ese hombre.

DOÑA LORETA: Siempre la inocencia resplandece.

PACHEQUIN: Pudiera no querer darte acogida. En tal caso, prométeme ser mía.

DOÑA LORETA: ¡Tuya, hasta la muerte!

PACHEQUIN: Te acompañaré para prevenir un arrebato de ese hombre demente.

DOÑA LORETA: ¡No expongas la vida por mí! ...

PACHEQUIN: Es deber que tengo.

Pachequín, muy jaque, se pone la gorra en la oreja y empuña el estoque. La tarasca sale delante con el pañuelo en los ojos. Sobre la copa negra de la higuera se espatarra el pelele en un círculo de luceros.

Escena sexta

En la sala dominguera, sobre el velador con tapete de ganchillo, el quinqué de porcelana azul ilumina el álbum de retratos. Pasa por la pared, gesticulante, la sombra de Don Friolera. Un ratón, a la boca de su agujero, arruga el hocico y curiosea la vitola de aquel adefesio con gorrilla de cuartel, babuchas moras, bragas azules de un uniforme viejo, y rayado chaleco de Bayona. El quinqué de porcelana translúcida tiene un temblor enclenque.

DON FRIOLERA: ¡Pim! ¡Pam! ¡Pum! ... ¡No me tiembla a mí la mano! Hecha justicia, me presento a mi Coronel: "Mi Coronel, ¿cómo se lava la honra?" Ya sé su respuesta. ¡Pim! ¡Pam! ¡Pum! ¡Listos! En el honor no puede haber nubes. Me presento voluntario a cumplir condena. ¡Mi Coronel, soy otro Teniente Capriles! Eran culpables, no soy un asesino. Si me correspode pena de ser fusilado, pido gracia para mandar el fuego: "¡Muchachos, firmes y a la cabeza! ¡Adiós, mis queridos compañeros! Tenéis esposas honradas, y debéis estimarlas. ¡No consintáis nunca el adulterio en el Cuerpo de Carabineros!" ¡Friolera! ¡Eran culpables! ¡Pagaron con su sangre! ¡No soy un asesino!

LORETTA: But I'm a wife and mother!

PACHEQUIN: I fear that man may take your life.

LORETTA: Our innocence shines as clear as day.

PACHEQUIN: He may be unwilling to take you back. In such an event, promise you'll be mine.

LORETTA: Yours till the day I die!

PACHEQUIN: I'll come with you in case that madman has another fit.

LORETTA: Don't put your life at risk for me!

PACHEQUIN: A man must do what a man must do.

Pachequín gallantly places his cap over his ear and clutches his narrow sword-stick. His floozie exits before him with her shawl over her eyes. In the blackness at the top of the fig-tree the scarecrow-like figure sticks out his limbs in a circle of stars.

Scene Six

In the parlour the light from the porcelain oil-lamp on the table with the crochet cover picks out the photograph album. The gesticulating shadow of Mr Punch moves up and down the wall. A mouse, at the entrance to its hole, wrinkles its nose as it peers at the outlandish figure wearing a military cap, moorish slippers, blue breeches from a worn-out uniform and a striped Bayonne waistcoat. The blue porcelain lamp flickers fitfully.

MR PUNCH: Take that! And that! And that!... Steady as a rock, my hand is! When I've carried out the death sentence, I'll appear before the Colonel: "Colonel, Sah!, how do we soldiers cleanse our honour?" I know what his answer will be. Bang! Bang! Bang! That's the way we do it! Atten...shun! We'll have no stains on our honour. I'm turning myself in to take my punishment. Sir, I've done a Lieutenant Hornblower! They were guilty, I'm no common murderer. If I'm to be shot, request permission to command the firing squad, Sah: "Steady now, lads, and aim at the head. Farewell, dear brothers-in-arms! You have virtuous wives, you should appreciate them. Adultery must never be tolerated in the Customs Corps!" Deary, deary me! They were guilty! They paid with their lives! I'm no common murderer!

Rechina la puerta y en el umbral aparece Doña Loreta. Tras ella, en la sombra del pasillo, se apunta la figura del barbero con el quepis sobre una ceja y la capa acandilada por el estoque. Doña Loreta cae de rodillas juntando las manos.

DOÑA LORETA: ¡Pascual!

DON FRIOLERA: ¿Conoces tu sentencia?

DOÑA LORETA: Pascualín, si dudas de mi inocencia, si me repudias de esposa, que sea de una manera decente y sin escándalo.

DON FRIOLERA: En España, la mujer que falta, tiene pena de la vida.

DOÑA LORETA: Pascual, nunca tu esposa dejó de guardarte la debida fidelidad.

DON FRIOLERA: ¡Pruebas! ¡Pruebas!

DOÑA LORETA: ¡También yo las pido, Pascual!

DON FRIOLERA: ¡Loreta, es preciso que resplandezca tu inocencia!

DOÑA LORETA: Como el propio sol resplandece. ¿Quién me acusa? ¡Un hombre bárbaro! ¡Un celoso demente! ¡Un turco sanguinario! ¡Mátame, pero no me calumnies!

DON FRIOLERA: ¿De donde vienes? Y ese hombre por qué te acompaña?

PACHEQUIN: Para testificar que tiene usted una perla por esposa. ¡Una heroína!

DON FRIOLERA: ¡Pruebas! ¡Pruebas!

PACHEQUIN: ¿No le satisface a usted el hecho de que un servidor se constituya en su domicilio para hacerle entrega de su señora?

DOÑA LORETA: ¿Qué respondes?

PACHEQUIN: Déjele usted que lo medite, Doña Loreta.

DOÑA LORETA: Ten un impulso generoso, Pascualín.

PACHEQUIN: Comprenda usted, mi Teniente, la razón de las cosas.

DON FRIOLERA: Pachequín, sal de esta casa. No puedo soportar tu presencia. Te concedo un plazo de cinco minutos.

PACHEQUIN: ¡Mi Teniente, es usted un dramático sempiterno!

DON FRIOLERA: Pachequín, dudo si eres un cínico o el primer caballero de España.

PACHEQUIN: Soy un romántico, mi Teniente.

DON FRIOLERA: Yo también, y te propongo un duelo a dos pasos en el cementerio.

DOÑA LORETA: ¿Vuelves a tus dudas?

DON FRIOLERA: Llámalas garfios infernales.

PACHEQUIN: Yo me retiro.

DON FRIOLERA: ¡El demonio te lleve!

DOÑA LORETA: ¡Qué proceder el de ese amigo, Pascual!

Hinges creak and Loretta appears in the doorway. Behind her, in the semi-darkness of the passage, the figure of the barber can be made out, his kepi over one eyebrow and a bulge in his cape caused by his sword-stick. Loretta falls to her knees, clasping her hands together.

LORETTA: Pascual!

MR PUNCH: Are you aware you've been sentenced to death?

LORETTA: Paskie, if you doubt my innocence, if you must reject me as a wife, at least do it decently, without any scandal.

MR PUNCH: Here in Spain the penalty for a wife who strays is death.

LORETTA: Pascual, I've always been a proper, faithful wife to you.

MR PUNCH: Proof! I must have proof!

LORETTA: What about you proving you love me!

MR PUNCH: Loretta, your innocence has to be clear beyond all shadow of doubt!

LORETTA: But it is, it's as clear as the sun in the sky. Who is it that accuses me? A brute of a man! A husband crazed with jealousy! A bloodthirsty Turk! Kill me if you will, but slander me, never!

MR PUNCH: Where have you just come from? And what's that man doing with you?

PACHEQUIN: I'm here as a witness in your wife's defence. She's an absolute jewel, a heroine!

MR PUNCH: Proof! I demand proof!

PACHEQUIN: Aren't you satisfied by the fact that the party of the first instance has made an appearance on your premises to effect due restitution of your lawful spouse?

LORETTA: There, see!

PACHEQUIN: Let him think about it, Loretta.

LORETTA: Have a heart, Paskie.

PACHEQUIN: Lieutenant Sir, there's a reasonable explanation for everything.

MR PUNCH: Pachequín, leave this house immediately. I refuse to tolerate your presence. You've got five minutes.

PACHEQUIN: Still the same old play-actor, Lieutenant Sir!

MR PUNCH: Pachequín, I can't work out whether you're a brazen liar or the most honourable gentleman in Spain.

PACHEQUIN: Me, I'm just an old-fashioned romantic, Lieutenant Sir.

MR PUNCH: So am I, and I challenge you to pistols at two paces in the graveyard.

LORETTA: Still at it with your suspicions?

MR PUNCH: Is that what you call them? They're more like hellish barbs in my flesh.

PACHEQUIN: I'm leaving.

MR PUNCH: The Devil take you!

LORETTA: He's behaving like a true friend, Pascual!

DON FRIOLERA: ¡No me subleves!

DOÑA LORETA: ¡Rencoroso!

DON FRIOLERA: ¡Es inaudito!

DOÑA LORETA: ¡Palabrotas, no, Pascual! ¡Eres un soldadote y no me respetas!

DON FRIOLERA: Me avistaré con ese hombre y le propondré un arreglo a tiros. Es la solución más honrosa.

DOÑA LORETA: ¡Y si te mata!

DON FRIOLERA: Te quedas viuda y libre.

DOÑA LORETA: Pascual, esas palabras son puñales que me traspasan. Pascual, yo jamás consentiré que expongas tu vida por una demencia.

DON FRIOLERA: No sé cómo podrás impedirlo.

DOÑA LORETA: ¡Me tomaré una pastilla de sublimado![1]

DON FRIOLERA: El sublimado de las boticas no mata.

DOÑA LORETA: ¡Una caja de cerillas!

DON FRIOLERA: Serán inútiles todos tus histerismos.

DOÑA LORETA: ¿Sigues de mala data para mí, Pascual? ¡Necesitas reposo!

DON FRIOLERA: ¡Déjame!

DOÑA LORETA: ¡Pascual, tendremos que divorciarnos si persistes en tus dudas! Estás haciendo de mí la Esposa Mártir.

DON FRIOLERA: ¡Quieres la libertad para volver al lado de ese hombre! Nos divorciaremos, pero entrarás en un convento de arrepentidas.

DOÑA LORETA: ¡Tirano!

DON FRIOLERA: ¡Has destruido mi vida!

DOÑA LORETA: Pascual, ¿por qué me haces desgraciada? Recógete, Pascual. Procura conciliar el sueño.

DON FRIOLERA: El sueño huyó de mis párpados.

DOÑA LORETA: ¡Pascual, ten juicio!

DON FRIOLERA: ¡Mi vida está acabada!

DOÑA LORETA: Pascual, tienes una hija, me tienes a mí ...

DON FRIOLERA: ¡Loreta, me has hecho dudar de todo!

DOÑA LORETA: Pascual, no seas injusto.

DON FRIOLERA: ¡Quisiera serlo!

Doña Loreta, desgarrado el gesto, temblona y rebotada el anca, flojo el corsé, sueltas las jaretas de las enaguas, sale corretona, y reaparece con una botella de anisete escarchado.

DOÑA LORETA: ¡Vaya, esto se acabó! Pascual, vamos a beber una copa juntos. Es el regalo de Curro Cadenas.

---

1   Corrosive sublimate (mercuric chloride), used, very diluted, as a disinfectant.

MR PUNCH: Stop this sedition!

LORETTA: You bitter, twisted man!

MR PUNCH: I'm absolutely flabbergasted!

LORETTA: Mind your language, Pascual! You're a rough brute of a soldier, you don't treat me with any respect!

MR PUNCH: I'll arrange a meeting with that man of yours and challenge him to settle it with pistols. It's the most honourable solution.

LORETTA: And what if he kills you!

MR PUNCH: You'll be a widow and free of me.

LORETTA: Pascual, your words are daggers in my heart. Pascual, I can never allow you to risk your life for a mad obsession.

MR PUNCH: Just try and stop me.

LORETTA: I'll swallow a disinfectant tablet!

MR PUNCH: The ones they sell at the chemist won't kill you.

LORETTA: I'll eat a whole box of matches!

MR PUNCH: None of your hysterical threats will make any difference.

LORETTA: Are you still in a bad mood with me, Pascual? What you need is some sleep!

MR PUNCH: Leave me be!

LORETTA: Pascual, if you don't forget these suspicions we'll have to get a divorce! The original wife and martyr had nothing on me.

MR PUNCH: You want your freedom so you can be with that man of yours! All right, you can have your divorce, but you'll go into a convent for fallen women.

LORETTA: You tyrant!

MR PUNCH: You've ruined my life!

LORETTA: Pascual, why do you keep upsetting me? Go to bed, Pascual. Try and get some sleep.

MR PUNCH: Nevermore will sleep come to my eyes.

LORETTA: Pascual, be sensible!

MR PUNCH: There's nothing left for me now!

LORETTA: Pascual, you've got your little daughter, you've got me ...

MR PUNCH: Loretta, because of you I can't believe in anything ever again!

LORETTA: Pascual, that's not fair.

MR PUNCH: Alas, it's only too true!

Loretta, wanton in her movements, her flesh quivering and her hips bouncing, her corset loose and her bloomer-strings unfastened, flounces out and comes back with a bottle of frosted anisette.

LORETTA: That's enough now! Pascual, we're going to have a drink together. It's the little something from Flash Frank Cadenas.

DON FRIOLERA: Yo no bebo.

DOÑA LORETA: Bebes, y vas a emborracharte conmigo.

DON FRIOLERA: ¡Contigo, jamas! ¡Te aborrezco!

DOÑA LORETA: Pues te emborrachas solo.

DON FRIOLERA: ¿Para olvidar?

DOÑA LORETA: Naturaca. ¡Bebe!

DON FRIOLERA: ¡No bebo!

DOÑA LORETA: ¡Te lo vierto por la cabeza!

DON FRIOLERA: ¡Espera!

El Teniente recibe la copa con mano temblona, y al apurarla, derrama un hilo de la mosca a la nuez.

DOÑA LORETA: ¡Otra!

DON FRIOLERA: ¿Intentas embriagarme?

DOÑA LORETA: Te hará bien.

DON FRIOLERA: Rechazo ese expediente.

DOÑA LORETA: ¡Otra, digo!

DON FRIOLERA: ¡Si con esto olvidase!

DOÑA LORETA: A lo menos te dormirás y descansaremos.

DON FRIOLERA: No me dormiré. ¡No puedo!

DOÑA LORETA: ¡Bebe!

DON FRIOLERA: ¿Cuántas van?

DOÑA LORETA: No lo sé, ¡bebe!

DON FRIOLERA: ¿Quién está oculto en aquella puerta?

DOÑA LORETA: ¡El gato!

DON FRIOLERA: ¿Cuántas van?

DOÑA LORETA: ¡Bebe!

DON FRIOLERA: Enciende una cerilla, Loreta. ¿Quién está oculto en aquella puerta? ¡No te escondas, miserable!

DOÑA LORETA: ¡Bebe!

DON FRIOLERA: ¡Es Pachequín! ¡Loreta, pon una sartén a la lumbre! ¡Vas a freírme los hígados de ese pendejo!

DOÑA LORETA: ¡No me asustes, Pascual!

DON FRIOLERA: ¡Y no tendrás más remedio que probar una tajada!

DOÑA LORETA: ¡Ya la cogiste!

DON FRIOLERA: ¡Ese Pachequín es un busca pendencias! ¿A qué fue ponerse tan gallo? ¿Duermes, Loreta? Responde. ¿Duermes?

DOÑA LORETA: Duermo.

DON FRIOLERA: Tú, con tu actitud, le diste alas. Responde, Loreta.

MR PUNCH: I won't drink it.
LORETTA: Go on, have a drink, get drunk with me.
MR PUNCH: With you? Never! I hate you!
LORETTA: Then get drunk on your own.
MR PUNCH: Why? To forget?
LORETTA: What else? Drink up!
MR PUNCH: I won't!
LORETTA: I'll tip it over your head if you don't!
MR PUNCH: Wait!

The Lieutenant takes the glass with a trembling hand and, as he drains it, a trickle runs from his chin to his Adam's apple.

LORETTA: Have another!
MR PUNCH: Are you trying to get me inebriated?
LORETTA: It'll do you good.
MR PUNCH: Application denied!
LORETTA: Come on, have another!
MR PUNCH: If only it could make me forget!
LORETTA: At least you'll sleep and we'll get some peace and quiet.
MR PUNCH: I won't sleep. I can't!
LORETTA: Drink up!
MR PUNCH: How many have I had?
LORETTA: No idea. Drink it!
MR PUNCH: Who's that hiding behind the door?
LORETTA: The cat!
MR PUNCH: How many have I had?
LORETTA: Drink up!
MR PUNCH: Light a match, Loretta. Who's that hiding behind the door? Come
            out, you bastard!
LORETTA: Drink!
MR PUNCH: It's Pachequín! Loretta, put the frying-pan on! You're going to
            fry up that little creep's liver for me!
LORETTA: Stop frightening me, Pascual!
MR PUNCH: And you're going to eat a slice, like it or not!
LORETTA: Stoned at last!
MR PUNCH: That Pachequín's a trouble-maker! What did he have to get so
            cocky for? Have you gone to sleep, Loretta? Answer me. You
            awake?
LORETTA: I'm asleep.
MR PUNCH: It was you leading him on that started him strutting and crowing,
            wasn't it? Answer me, Loretta.

DOÑA LORETA: Me he quedado sorda de un aire.
DON FRIOLERA: ¡Impúdica!
DOÑA LORETA: ¡Mierda!

Doña Loreta toma el quinqué, y dejando la sala a oscuras, se mete por la puerta de escape pintada de azul, recogidas sobre una cadera las sueltas enaguas.

DON FRIOLERA: Si tú ocupas la cama matrimonial, yo dormiré en la esterilla.
DOÑA LORETA: ¡Duerme debajo de la escalera, como San Alejo![1]
DON FRIOLERA: ¡Loretita! Donde hay amor, hay celos. No te enojes, pichona, con tu pichón. ¿Duermes, Loretita?

Escena séptima

El billar de Doña Calixta: sala baja con pinturas absurdas, de un sentimiento popular y dramático. Contrabandistas de trabuco y manta jerezana; manolas de bolero y calañés, con ojos asesinos; picadores y toros, alaridos del rojo y del amarillo. Curro Cadenas toma café en la mesa más cercana al mostrador, y conversa con la dueña, que sobre un fondo de botillería destaca su busto propincuo, de cuarentona.

DOÑA CALIXTA: ¿Currillo, ha oído usted esa voz de que expulsan de la milicia a Don Friolera?
CURRO: Usted siempre estará mejor enterada, Doña Calixta.
DOÑA CALIXTA: Pues no lo estoy.
CURRO: Como tiene usted de huésped al Teniente Rovirosa.
DOÑA CALIXTA: Ese señor, para guardar un secreto, es la rúbrica de un escribano.
CURRO: ¿No están reunidos en el los tres Tenientes?
DOÑA CALIXTA: Con dos barajas.
CURRO: De ahí saldrá la bomba.
DOÑA CALIXTA: Sentiré la desgracia de Don Friolera. ¡Era un sujeto muy decente!
CURRO: Había dado un cambiazo.
DOÑA CALIXTA: Otro vendrá que le haga bueno.

---

1 St. Alexis (4th c. A. D.), who disguised himself as a beggar and slept under the stairs rather than sully his purity by consummating an arranged marriage.

LORETTA: Can't hear a thing you're saying.
MR PUNCH: Trollop!
LORETTA: Bollocks!

Loretta picks up the lamp and, her unfastened bloomers gathered over one hip, makes her escape through the blue-painted door, leaving the room in darkness.

MR PUNCH: If you're sleeping in our bed, I'm going to sleep on the settee.
LORETTA; Sleep under the stairs in a hair shirt for all I care!
MR PUNCH: Lottikins, it's only love that makes me so jealous. Don't be angry with your little pigeon, my lovey-dove. You asleep, Lottikins?

Scene Seven

Calixta's billiard saloon. A ground-floor room with absurd paintings in a popular, dramatic style: smugglers with muskets and Jerez cloaks; molls in boleros and broad-rimmed hats, with eyes that can kill; picadors and bulls, a riot in red and yellow. Flash Frank Cadenas drinks his coffee at the nearest table to the counter and converses with the proprietress, who, against the background of the drinks shelves, thrusts out her hefty, forty-year-old's bust.

CALIXTA: Frankie-boy, have you heard the rumour that they're throwing Mr Punch out of the service?
FLASH FRANK: You're bound to be more in the know than me, Calixta.
CALIXTA: Well, not in this case.
FLASH FRANK: Seeing as how your lodger here is Lieutenant Rovirosa ...
CALIXTA: That particular individual keeps his cards very close to his chest.
FLASH FRANK: Aren't the three Lieutenants holding a meeting upstairs?
CALIXTA: And they've dug in for a long session.
FLASH FRANK: That's where the bombshell will come from.
CALIXTA: I feel really sorry for Mr Punch and the bad time he's having. He was a good skin, all in all.
FLASH FRANK: He'd changed for the worse, though.
CALIXTA: He might still change back for the better.

CURRO: En general, la clase de oficiales es decente. El mal está en los altos
espacios. ¡Allí no entienden si no es por miles de pesetas! ¡La
parranda de los guarismos es aquello!

DOÑA CALIXTA: ¡Si usted no pisa por esos suelos alfombrados!

CURRO: ¡Qué sabe usted los palacios donde yo entro! Un servidor ha dejado
por las alturas más pápiros que tiene el Banco de España.

DOÑA CALIXTA: Currillo, es usted un telescopio contando.

CURRO: Tómelo usted a guasa.

DOÑA CALIXTA: ¿Tiene usted fábrica de moneda?

CURRO: ¡Así es! El Gobierno me ha concedido el monopolio de los duros
sevillanos.[1]

DOÑA CALIXTA: ¡Para hacerse rico!

CURRO: No tanto. La flor del negocio se la llevan las acciones liberadas.[2]

DOÑA CALIXTA: ¡Guasista! Cállese un momento. ¡Arriba hablan recio!

CURRO: Me parece que disputan por una jugada.

*El Teniente Don Friolera, escoltado por un perrillo con borla en la punta del
rabo, entra en la sala de los billares. Zancudo, amarillento y flaco, se llega al
mostrador, bordeando las grandes mesas verdes, y saluda, alzada la mano a la
visera del ros.*

DON FRIOLERA: Doña Calixta, una copa de aguardiente, que no voy a pagar.

DOÑA CALIXTA: Tiene usted crédito.

DON FRIOLERA: Salí de casa sin tabaco y sin numerario. Tuvimos una nube
en el matrimonio, y no he querido pedirle a mi señora la llave de
la gaveta.

CURRO: Doña Calixta, si aquí me autoriza, esta copa la paga un servidor.

DON FRIOLERA: Currillo, no te subas a la gavia, pero ésta prefiero debérsela
a Doña Calixta.

CURRO: Con lo cual quiere decirse que tomará usted otra, mi Teniente.

DON FRIOLERA: ¡Bueno!

*Con gesto confidencial, se aparta al fondo de una ventana, y hace señas al otro
para que le siga. Curro Cadenas toma una expresión de sorna.*

DON FRIOLERA: ¡Mira, hijo, bebo para sacarme un clavo del pensamiento!

CURRO: ¡Ni una palabra más!

DON FRIOLERA: ¿Tú me comprendes?

CURRO: ¡Totalmente!

---

1 A reference to the discovery of counterfeit five-peseta coins which, since they
had the same metal value as the genuine ones, were allegedly melted down and
reissued by the Bank of Spain.

2 Special shares which are made available to company directors (and their banking
cronies) at a nominal price and under highly favourable conditions.

FLASH FRANK: Officers, in general, are a decent bunch. The problem lies with the top brass. They won't tip you the wink unless there's a percentage in it for them! That's where the real money's made!

CALIXTA: Well, you certainly don't move in such distinguished circles!

FLASH FRANK: What do you know about where I've had occasion to hang my hat? Yours truly has made more deposits amongst the upper crust than you'd find in the coffers of the Bank of Spain.

CALIXTA: Well, Frankie-boy, you can certainly spin them bigger than any spider!

FLASH FRANK: Take it as a joke, if you like.

CALIXTA: Have you got your own coin factory, then?

FLASH FRANK: Yes, didn't you know? The Government's given me exclusive rights to the mint in Seville

CALIXTA: So you can act the swell!

FLASH FRANK: Not that much. It's the insider dealing that creams off the best part of the profits.

CALIXTA: Pull the other one! Hush a moment. They're raising their voices upstairs!

FLASH FRANK: They'll be arguing the toss.

Mr Punch enters the billiard saloon, escorted by a little dog with a tassel on the end of its tail. Lanky, jaundiced and lean, he walks up to the bar, skirting the big green tables and touches his cap in salute.

MR PUNCH: A glass of brandy, Calixta, which you'll have to put on the slate.

CALIXTA: Your credit's good here.

MR PUNCH: I've left my cash and fags at home. Me and the wife have had a bit of a barney and I felt disinclined to ask the good lady for the key to the money-box.

FLASH FRANK: If it's not out of order, Calixta, yours truly will pay for that drink.

MR PUNCH: Don't take it amiss, Frankie-boy, but I'd rather owe Calixta this one.

FLASH FRANK: Which merely means to say, Lieutenant, that the next one's on me.

MR PUNCH: Fair enough!

As if wishing to confide, he moves off towards the window and beckons the other to follow. Flash Frank Cadenas assumes a knowing expression.

MR PUNCH: Look lad, I'm drinking to take a weight off my mind.

FLASH FRANK: Enough said.

MR PUNCH: You get me?

FLASH FRANK: Absolutely!

DON FRIOLERA: ¡Tengo el corazón lacerado! ¡Mi mujer me ha salido rana!

CURRO: ¡Siento la ocurrencia!

DON FRIOLERA: ¿Ya lo sabías, verdad?

CURRO: Andaba ese runrún. Fúmese usted ese tabaco, mi Teniente.

DON FRIOLERA: Estoy en ayunas, y puede marearme. ¡Engañado por el amigo y por la depositaria de mi honor!

CURRO: La vida está llena de esos casos. ¡Hay que tener otra conformidad, mi Teniente!

DON FRIOLERA: ¿Para qué nacemos?

CURRO: Para rabiar. Somos las consecuencias de los buenos ratos habidos entre nuestros padres. ¿No se fuma usted el veguero?

DON FRIOLERA: Dame una cerilla. ¡Gracias! Mira cómo me tiembla la mano.

CURRO: Eso son nervios.

DON FRIOLERA: ¡Es el fruto del puñal que llevo en el corazón!

CURRO: Mi Teniente, ande usted con pupila, que los señores oficiales están reunidos en el piso alto.

DON FRIOLERA: Desprecio el vil metal, hijo mío. ¡Ya sabes que nunca he sido interesado! Déjalos a ellos que prevariquen, sin acordarse de este veterano.

CURRO: A lo que se mienta, no va por ahí el motivo de esa reunión.

DON FRIOLERA: ¡A mí, plin! Tengo el corazón lacerado.

CURRO: De esa reunión pudiera salir para usted una novedad nada buena. Mi Teniente, se corre que le forman a usted Tribunal.

DON FRIOLERA: ¡Friolera! ¿Que me forman Tribunal? ¿Y por qué?

CURRO: ¡Me extraña verle tan ciego! Parece que por sus pleitos familiares.

DON FRIOLERA: En ellos, solamente yo puedo ser juez.

CURRO: Así debía ser. Una pregunta, mi Teniente.

DON FRIOLERA: Venga.

CURRO: ¿De tener que solicitar el retiro, cambiaría usted de residencia?

DON FRIOLERA: No lo he pensado.

CURRO: Le debo a usted una explicación, Don Pascual. La casa que usted habita, a mi señora le hace tilín. ¡Es una jaula muy alegre!

DON FRIOLERA: ¡Maldita sea!

Don Friolera apura la copa servida en el mostrador, se encasqueta el ros, y con las manos metidas en los bolsillos del capote sale a la calle, silbando al perrillo que le sigue, moviendo la borla del rabo.

MR PUNCH: My heart's in torment! The wife's done the dirty on me!

FLASH FRANK: Please accept my condolences.

MR PUNCH: You already knew about it, didn't you?

FLASH FRANK: There's been a rumour to that effect. Have a fag, Lieutenant.

MR PUNCH: It might make me dizzy on an empty stomach. Stabbed in the back by a friend and the depositary of my honour!

FLASH FRANK: Life's full of stories like that, Lieutenant. We've got to learn to live with these things.

MR PUNCH: What do we come into this world for?

FLASH FRANK: To go stark raving mad. We're nothing more than the result of the good times had by our parents. Are you sure you won't have a weed?

MR PUNCH: Give me a light. Thanks. Look how my hand's shaking.

FLASH FRANK: That's nerves.

MR PUNCH: It's the fruit of the dagger embedded in my heart!

FLASH FRANK: Mind how you go, Lieutenant, your fellow officers are holding a business meeting upstairs.

MR PUNCH: I abhor the muck they call money, lad. You know I've never got mixed up in anything like that. Let them get on with it and leave this old soldier completely out of it.

FLASH FRANK: The word is that it's not that type of business that's on the agenda.

MR PUNCH: I couldn't give a monkey's! My heart has been torn to shreds.

FLASH FRANK: This meeting might turn out to be nothing but bad news for you. Rumour has it, Lieutenant, that they're court-martialling you.

MR PUNCH: Deary, deary me! Court-martialling me! Why?

FLASH FRANK: Your blindness amazes me! The motive seems to be your domestic dispute.

MR PUNCH: Only I can be the judge and jury of all that.

FLASH FRANK: That's the way it ought to be. A word in your ear, Lieutenant.

MR PUNCH: Proceed.

FLASH FRANK: If you were forced into retirement, would you be moving house?

MR PUNCH: I've not given it any thought.

FLASH FRANK: I owe you an explanation, Pascual. My missus would be tickled pink with the house you're in; it's a jolly little lair.

MR PUNCH: To hell with it!

Mr Punch drains the glass and leaves it on the bar. He pulls down his cap and goes into the street with his hands deep in the pockets of his cape. He whistles the dog to follow him and it wags the tassel on its tail

DOÑA CALIXTA: Parece mochales.

CURRO: Completamente.

DOÑA CALIXTA: Siento su desgracia. Era un apreciable sujeto.

CURRO: Un viva la Virgen.

DOÑA CALIXTA: Doña Loreta merecía ser emplumada.

Curro Cadenas se acerca al mostrador y pomposo deja caer un machacante haciéndolo saltar. Espera la vuelta dando lumbre a un habano, y bajo el reflejo de la cerilla, su cara es luna llena. Recibido el dinero, se lo guarda con un guiño.

CURRO: Doña Calixta, tengo en cierto lugar una pacotilla de género inglés, y cornea sobre esa querencia un toro marrajo. Doña Calixta, usted podría muletearlo.

DOÑA CALIXTA: No me penetro.

CURRO: En cuanto le apunte el nombre, está usted más que penetrada.

DOÑA CALIXTA: Acaso.

CURRO: Yo sabría corresponder ...

DOÑA CALIXTA: Puede.

CURRO: No se ponga usted enigmática, Doña Calixta.

DOÑA CALIXTA: ¡Currillo, usted anda en muy malos pasos!

CURRO: Hay que ganarse el manró, y todos nos debemos ayuda mutua, Doña Calixta. Nosotros, los que con sudores y trabajos hemos sabido juntar unas pesetas, habíamos de sindicarnos como hace el proletariado.

DOÑA CALIXTA: ¡Currillo, el buey suelto bien se lame!

CURRO: Doña Calixta, hoy todo está cambiado, y hasta son mentira los refranes. Vea usted como el obrero se conchaba para subir los jornales. ¡Qué va! Hasta el propio Gobierno se conchaba para sacarnos los cuartos en contribuciones y Aduanas.

DOÑA CALIXTA: Esas no son novedades.

CURRO: ¿Doña Calixta, quiere usted que hablemos sin macaneos?

DOÑA CALIXTA: Yo bailo al son que me tocan.

CURRO: Pues oído al repique: hay a la vista un negocio, si usted camela al Teniente Rovirosa. ¿Hace?

DOÑA CALIXTA: Apenas llevamos trato. Buenos días. Buenas noches. El, arriba o en sus guardias. Yo, aquí. La cuenta a fin de mes. Viene usted mal informado, Currillo.

CURRO: Otra cosa me habían contado.

DOÑA CALIXTA: Hay lenguas muy embusteras.

CALIXTA: He's lost his marbles.

FLASH FRANK: Every last one.

CALIXTA: I feel sorry for him. He wasn't a bad old skin.

FLASH FRANK: A canny lad.

CALIXTA: Loretta deserves to be tarred and feathered.

Flash Frank Cadenas swaggers up to the bar and drops a tanner on it, spinning it round. He waits for his change and lights up a Havana cigar. In the reflection from his match his face is a full moon. He takes his money and puts it away with a wink.

FLASH FRANK: Calixta, I have in my possession – and not a million miles from here – a consignment of English merchandise. But there's a rather mischievous bloodhound sniffing around where it's stashed and you, Calixta, could throw him off the scent.

CALIXTA: I don't get it.

FLASH FRANK: As soon as I give you his name, you'll do more than get it.

CALIXTA: That's as maybe.

FLASH FRANK: I could make it worth your while.

CALIXTA: Perhaps.

FLASH FRANK: Now don't get cute about it, Calixta.

CALIXTA: You, Frankie-boy, are up to no good!

FLASH FRANK: We've all got to earn our crust and it helps if we scratch one another's backs a bit. Especially in the case of those of us who, by the sweat of our brow, have put a few bob together. We should form a union like the working class are doing.

CALIXTA: Be your own boss and don't give a toss, that's what I say, Frankie-boy.

FLASH FRANK: It's all changed these days, Calixta, and even the old sayings don't mean a thing any more. Haven't you seen how workers stick together to get a wage rise. Jesus, even the Government closes ranks to filch our hard-earned cash with taxes and excise duties!

CALIXTA: There's nothing new in that.

FLASH FRANK: Calixta, would you prefer me not to beat about the bush?

CALIXTA: I dance to whatever tune the piper plays.

FLASH FRANK: Enough said; I'll lead and you follow. We might be able to do a little business if you could use your charms on Lieutenant Rovirosa. Know what I mean?

CALIXTA: We hardly have anything to do with each other; just the odd "Good morning" or "Good night". He's either upstairs or on duty, I'm down here and the bill's paid at the end of the month. You're well off the mark there, Frankie-boy.

FLASH FRANK: That's not what I've been told.

CALIXTA: There's a lot of malicious gossip about.

CURRO: No ha sido en desdoro, Doña Calixta.

DOÑA CALIXTA: ¿Qué le habían contado?

CURRO: Que el Teniente es hombre de gusto.

DOÑA CALIXTA: ¡Y que me deshace la cama!

CURRO: No, señora. Que usted le da achares.

DOÑA CALIXTA: Menos mal.

CURRO: Y lo he creído, porque usted es muy inhumana.

DOÑA CALIXTA: ¿Me juzgaba usted otra Doña Loreta?

CURRO: Nunca sería el mismo caso. Usted es libre, Doña Calixta.

DOÑA CALIXTA: Nunca se es libre para pecar.

CURRO: Hacer hijos no es pecado.

DOÑA CALIXTA: ¿Y quién los mantiene?

CURRO: El Erario Público.

DOÑA CALIXTA: Eso será en las Repúblicas.

CURRO: En toda la Europa. Y por las señales, a pesar del oscurantismo, no tardará en España.

DOÑA CALIXTA: Aquí no estamos para esas modas de extranjis.

CURRO: Por de pronto, ya le han dado mulé a Dato.

DOÑA CALIXTA: Unos asesinos.

CURRO: Conforme. Mis ideas también son antirrevolucionarias. El que tiene un negocio y cuatro patacones, no puede ser un ácrata. Pero se guipa alguna cosa, y comprendo que el orden social se tambalea. Doña Calixta, los negocios están muy malos. Ahora hablan de suprimir las Aduanas, y a nosotros es matarnos. Si todos los artículos entran libremente, se acabó el contrabando. ¿Qué hace usted? Poner una bomba.

DOÑA CALIXTA: ¡Yo, no!

CURRO: Porque usted ya se apaña retirada del matuteo.

DOÑA CALIXTA: ¡A Dios gracias!

CURRO: Acuérdese usted de cuando andaba en estos trotes, y saque un ánima del Purgatorio.

DOÑA CALIXTA: Le rezaré un rosario.

CURRO: ¡Quiere usted cegar a su alojado con dos veraguas?

DOÑA CALIXTA: ¿Dos veraguas son cuarenta machacantes?

CURRO: Propiamente.

FLASH FRANK: It was nothing to your detriment, Calixta.

CALIXTA: What have you been told, then?

FLASH FRANK: That the Lieutenant is a man of good taste.

CALIXTA: And leaves his boots under my bed!

FLASH FRANK: Not at all. Rather that you give him the cold shoulder.

CALIXTA: A good job, too.

FLASH FRANK: I believed it, because you're a hard woman, Calixta.

CALIXTA: Did you take me for another Loretta?

FLASH FRANK: It wouldn't be the same thing. You, Calixta, are a woman who is foot-loose and fancy-free.

CALIXTA: A woman is never free to sin.

FLASH FRANK: Making babies is no sin.

CALIXTA: And who'll feed and clothe them?

FLASH FRANK: The State.

CALIXTA: That may be the way it is in a republic.

FLASH FRANK: In the whole of Europe. And from what I see, it won't be long till it's the same in Spain in spite of our unwillingness to change.

CALIXTA: We're not ready here for those trendy foreign ways.

FLASH FRANK: I'm not so sure. They certainly got rid of Dato[1] with a bang.

CALIXTA: Murderers! Terrorists!

FLASH FRANK: I agree. My ideas are just as anti-revolutionary. No-one who's built up a small business and got a couple of bob together can be an anarchist. But there are one or two things catch your eye and I've come to realise that society as we know it is teetering on the brink. Business has never been worse, Calixta. Now they're even talking about doing away with customs duty and that would be the ruination of us. If all merchandise could enter the country free, gratis and for nothing, then that would be the end for smuggling. What do you do? Plant a bomb.

CALIXTA: Not me!

FLASH FRANK: Because these days you earn a living outside our unofficial import industry.

CALIXTA: Thanks be to God!

FLASH FRANK: Just think back to when you had a finger in that particular pie, and help a poor soul out of Purgatory.

CALIXTA: I'll say a little prayer for you.

FLASH FRANK: Will you lead your lodger on for a pair of ponies?

CALIXTA: A pair of ponies? What's that, half a monkey?

FLASH FRANK: The very same.

1 Eduardo Dato, leader of the Conservative Party, was Prime Minister when he was assassinated by anarchists in 1921.

DOÑA CALIXTA: ¡Me los tira a la cara! ¡Ni que fuera un pelanas! Llegue usted a la corrida completa.
CURRO: No da el negocio para tanto.
DOÑA CALIXTA: ¡Miau!

Reaparece Don Friolera, el aire distraído, los ojos tristes, gesto y visajes de maniático. Entra furtivo, y se sienta en un rincón. El perrillo salta sobre el mugriento terciopelo del diván y se acomoda a su lado. Acude Barallocas, el mozo del cafetín.

BARALLOCAS: ¿Desea usted algo?
DON FRIOLERA: ¡Un veneno!

Barallocas, con gesto conciliador, pone sobre la mesa un servicio de café, y con la punta de la servilleta ahuyenta al perrillo del refugio del diván. Se pega en el labio la colilla que lleva en la oreja, enciende, humea y ocupa el puesto del perrillo, al lado de Don Friolera.

BARALLOCAS: ¡Hay que ser filósofo!
DON FRIOLERA: ¡Pues yo no lo soy!
BARALLOCAS: ¡Mal hecho! En España vivimos muy atrasados. Somos víctimas del clero. No se inculca la filosofía en los matrimonios, como se hace en otros países.
DON FRIOLERA: ¿Te refieres a la ley del divorcio?
BARALLOCAS: ¡Ya nos hemos entendido!

Barallocas guiña un ojo, y se levanta para acudir a la mesa donde acaban de sentarse el Niño del Melonar, Curro Cadenas y Nelo el Peneque. El perrillo recobra de un salto su puesto en el diván, y sacude el terciopelo con la borla del rabo.

CALIXTA: And is that all you can come up with? What do you take him for,
        some type of cheapskate? Hit me with the full Monty!
FLASH FRANK: I'm afraid that the old coffers won't stretch to that.
CALIXTA: Knickers!

*Mr Punch enters, his mind elsewhere, his eyes sad, with the appearance and
gestures of a lunatic. He steals in and sits in a corner. The little dog springs
onto the grimy velvet of the divan and settles down by his side. Barallocas, the
waiter, comes up to him.*

BARALLOCAS: What can I get you?
MR PUNCH: Poison!

*Barallocas, with a conciliatory gesture, puts a coffee-service on the table and
shoos the dog from its haven on the divan with the end of his serviette. He
sticks the dimp from behind his ear onto his bottom lip, lights it, has a drag and
sits in the dog's place beside Mr Punch.*

BARALLOCAS: You've got to be philosophical about it.
MR PUNCH: Well, I'm not!
BARALLOCAS: That's unfortunate. We're so far behind here in Spain. The
            Church has got us right where it wants us. There's no philosophy
            behind marriage as there is in other countries.
MR PUNCH: Are you refering to divorce?
BARALLOCAS: You get my meaning!

*Barallocas winks and gets up to serve the table where the Cantaloupe Kid, Flash
Frank Cadenas and Manny the Jug-head have just sat down. The little dog jumps
back onto its place on the divan and rustles the velvet with the tassel on its tail.*

Escena octava

Una sala con miradores que avistan a la marina. Sobre la consola, grandes caracoles sonoros y conchas perleras. El espejo, bajo un tul. En las paredes, papel con quioscos de mandarines, escalinatas y esquifes, lagos azules entre adormideras. La sierpe de un acordeón, al pie de la consola. En la cristalera del mirador, toman café y discuten tres señores oficiales. Levitines azules, pantalones potrosos, calvas lucientes, un feliz aspecto de relojeros. Conduce la discusión Don Lauro Rovirosa, que tiene un ojo de cristal, y cuando habla, solamente mueve un lado de la cara. Es Teniente veterano graduado de Capitán. Los otros dos, muy diversos de aspecto entre sí, son, sin embargo, de un parecido obsesionante, como acontece con esas parejas matrimoniales, de viejos un poco ridículos. Don Gabino Campero, filarmónico y orondo, está en el grupo de los gatos. Don Mateo Cardona, con sus ojos saltones y su boca de oreja a oreja, en el de las ranas.

EL TENIENTE ROVIROSA: Para formar juicio, hay que fiscalizar los hechos. Se trata de condenar a un compañero de armas, a un hermano, que podríamos decir. Acaso nos veamos en la obligación de formular una sentencia dura, pero justa. Comienzo por advertir a mis queridos compañeros que, en puntos de honor, me pronuncio contra todos los sentimentalismos.

EL TENIENTE CAMPERO: ¡En absoluto conforme! Pero, a mi ver, deseo constatar que la justicia no excluye la clemencia.

EL TENIENTE CARDONA: Hay que obligarle a pedir la absoluta. El Ejército no quiere cabrones.

EL TENIENTE ROVIROSA: ¡Evidente!

Don Lauro rubrica con un gesto tan terrible, que se le salta el ojo de cristal. De un zarpazo lo recoge rodante y trompicante en el mármol del velador, y se lo incrusta en la órbita.

EL TENIENTE CARDONA: Se trata del honor de todos los oficiales, puesto en entredicho por un Teniente cuchara.

EL TENIENTE CAMPERO: ¡Protesto! El cuartel es tan escuela de pundonor como las Academias. Yo procedo de la clase de tropa, y no toleraría que mi señora me adornase la frente. Se habla, sin

Scene Eight

A room with bay windows looking out over the harbour. On a dresser, some large conches and pearl-oyster shells. A mirror with tulle curtains. Wallpaper with a pattern of mandarins' kiosks, flights of steps, skiffs, blue lakes glimpsed between poppy-flowers. The serpent-shape of an accordion at the foot of the dresser. In the glass-framed bay window three officers-and-gentlemen are drinking coffee and holding a discussion. Blue jackets, breeches baggy at the crotch, gleaming bald heads, an air of cheerful watchmakers. Leading the debate is Lieutenant Lauro Rovirosa, who has a glass eye and moves only one side of his face when he speaks. He is a veteran Lieutenant-Captain. The other two, although of different appearance, have that obsessive similarity which is found in certain married couples who become slightly ridiculous as they get older. Lieutenant Gabino Campero, portly in shape and successful in his dealings, belongs to the cat family. Lieutenant Mateo Cardona, with his bulging eyes and ear-to-ear mouth, is of the frog tribe.

LIEUTENANT ROVIROSA: In order duly to constitute these proceedings, it is first necessary to establish the facts. We are gathered here to pass judgement on a comrade in arms, a brother, we might say. It may be our painful duty to decide on a just but severe punishment. To begin with, I wish to put on record, before my fellow officers, that in questions of honour I am categorically against any lily-livered sentimentality.
LIEUTENANT CAMPERO: Hear! Hear! But, for my part, I would like to point out that justice does not exclude mercy.
LIEUTENANT CARDONA: Make him put in for an absolute discharge. The Army has no room for bloody cuckolds.
LIEUTENANT ROVIROSA: Hear! Hear!
Lieutenant Lauro Rovirosa emphasises his words with so violent a gesture that his glass eye jumps out. He snatches it up with his claw as it bounces and rolls on the marble top of the coffee table, and sticks it back in its socket.

LIEUTENANT CARDONA: The fact is, the honour of every single officer has been put on the line by one squaddie lieutenant.
LIEUTENANT CAMPERO: Objection! The barrack-room is as strict a school of honour as your military academies. I came up from the ranks myself and there's no way I'd let my missus put one over on me. You seem to forget that the greatest military minds have always

recordar que las mejores cabezas militares siempre han salido de la clase de tropa: ¡Prim, pistolo! ¡Napoleón, pistolo! ...

EL TENIENTE CARDONA: ¡Sooo! Napoleón era procedente de la Academia de Artillería.

EL TENIENTE CAMPERO: ¡Puede ser! Pero el General Morillo, que le dio en la cresta, procedía de la clase de tropa y había sido mozo en un molino.

EL TENIENTE ROVIROSA: ¡Como el Rey de Nápoles, el famoso General Murat!

EL TENIENTE CAMPERO: Tengo leído alguna cosa de ese General. ¡Un tío muy bragado! ¡Napoleón le tenía miedo!

EL TENIENTE CARDONA: ¡Tanto como eso, Teniente Campero! ¡Miedo el Ogro de Córcega!

EL TENIENTE CAMPERO: Viene en la Historia.

EL TENIENTE CARDONA: No la he leído.

EL TENIENTE ROVIROSA:A mí, personalmente, los franceses me empalagan.

EL TENIENTE CARDONA: Demasiados cumplimientos.

EL TENIENTE ROVIROSA: Pero hay que reconocerles valentía. ¡Por algo son latinos, como nosotros!

EL TENIENTE CARDONA: Desde que hay mundo, los españoles les hemos pegado siempre a los gabachos.

EL TENIENTE ROVIROSA: ¡Y es natural! ¡Y se explica! ¡Y se comprende perfectamente! Nosotros somos moros y latinos. Los primeros soldados, según Lord Wellington. ¡Un inglés!

EL TENIENTE CAMPERO: A mi parecer, lo que mas tenemos es sangre mora. Se ve en los ataques a la bayoneta.

El Teniente Don Lauro Rovirosa alza y baja una ceja, la mano puesta sobre el ojo de cristal por si ocurre que se le antoje dispararse.

EL TENIENTE ROVIROSA: ¡Evidente! Somos muchas sangres, pero prepondera la africana. Siempre nos han mirado con envidia otros pueblos, y hemos tenido lluvia de invasores. Pero todos, al cabo

come up through the ranks. Prim,[1] an infantryman! Napoleon, an infantryman!

LIEUTENANT CARDONA: Steady on there! Napoleon was a graduate of the Artillery Academy.

LIEUTENANT CAMPERO: That's as may be, but General Morillo,[2] who gave him a drubbing, he rose from the ranks, and even worked in a mill when he was a lad.

LIEUTENANT ROVIROSA: Just like the King of Naples, the famous General Murat![3]

LIEUTENANT CAMPERO: I've read a thing or two about your General Murat. Real balls that guy had! Even Napoleon was scared of him!

LIEUTENANT CARDONA: That's a bit much, Lieutenant Campero! The Ogre of Corsica, scared?

LIEUTENANT CAMPERO: It's all there in the history books.

LIEUTENANT CARDONA: Well, I've never read them.

LIEUTENANT ROVIROSA: Personally, I find the French a bit hard to swallow.

LIEUTENANT CARDONA: Too many pleases and thank-yous.

LIEUTENANT ROVIROSA: But they're courageous, you've got to admit that. They're not Latins like us for nothing!

LIEUTENANT CARDONA: Ever since the world began, we Spaniards have always stuffed the Froggies.

LIEUTENANT ROVIROSA: What do you expect? It's easy to see why! It's only natural! We Spaniards are descendants of the Moors and the Romans. We make the best soldiers there are, Lord Wellington said so, and he was English!

LIEUTENANT CAMPERO: In my opinion, we have more Moorish blood in us. It comes out in our bayonet attacks.

Lieutenant Lauro Rovirosa raises and lowers one eyebrow, his hand covering his glass eye in case it gets the urge to pop out again.

LIEUTENANT ROVIROSA: That's right! We are a mixture of many races, but the African strain is the strongest. Other nations have always envied us, that's why we've been invaded time after time. But after

---

1 General Prim was War Minister in the Provisional Government of 1870 when he was assassinated.

2 Morillo, a shepherd in his youth, distinguished himself as a guerrilla leader in the struggle against the French occupation of Spain. He subsequently gained notoriety by the ferocity of his attempts to repress independence movements in South America.

3 Napoleon's brother-in-law and king of Naples during the period 1808-1814. He was defeated and executed in 1815.

de llevar algún tiempo viviendo bajo este hermoso sol, acabaron
por hacerse españoles.

EL TENIENTE CARDONA: Lo que está ocurriendo actualmente con los
ingleses de Gibraltar.

EL TENIENTE CAMPERO: Y en Marruecos. Allí no se oye hablar más que
árabe y español.

EL TENIENTE CARDONA: ¿Tagalo, no?

EL TENIENTE CAMPERO: Algún moro del interior. Español es lo más que
allí se habla.

EL TENIENTE CARDONA: Yo había aprendido alguna cosa de tagalo en Joló.
Ya lo llevo olvidado: *Tanbu*, que quiere decir puta. *Nital budila*:
hijo de mala madre. *Bede tuki pan pan bata*: ¡voy a romperte los
cuernos!

EL TENIENTE ROVIROSA: ¡Al parecer, posee usted a la perfección el tagalo!

EL TENIENTE CARDONA: ¡Lo más indispensable para la vida!

EL TENIENTE ROVIROSA: ¡Evidente! A mí se me ha olvidado lo poco que
sabía, e hice toda la campaña en Mindanao.

EL TENIENTE CARDONA: Yo he pasado cinco años en Joló. ¡Los mejores de
mi vida!

EL TENIENTE ROVIROSA: No todos podemos decir lo mismo. Ultramar ha
sido negocio para los altos mandos y para los sargentos de oficinas
... Mindanao tiene para mí mal recuerdo. Enviudé, y he perdido el
ojo derecho de la picadura de un mosquito.

EL TENIENTE CARDONA: La Isla de Joló ha sido para mí un paraíso. Cinco
años sin un mal dolor de cabeza y sin reservarme de comer, beber
y lo que cuelga.

EL TENIENTE CAMPERO: ¡Las batas de quince años son muy aceptables!

EL TENIENTE CARDONA: ¡De primera! Yo las daba un baño, les ponía una
camisa de nipis, y como si fuesen princesas.

*Su risa estremece los cristales del mirador, la ceniza del cigarro le vuela sobre las
barbas, la panza se infla con regocijo saturnal. Bailan en el velador las tazas del
café, salta el canario en la jaula y se sujeta su ojo de cristal el Teniente Don
Lauro Rovirosa.*

EL TENIENTE CAMPERO: ¡Qué tío sibarita!

EL TENIENTE CARDONA: ¡Aun de alegría me crispo al recordar su tesoro!

EL TENIENTE ROVIROSA: Permítanme ustedes que les recuerde el objetivo
que aquí nos reune. Un primordial deber nos impone velar por el
decoro de la familia militar, como ha dicho en cierta ocasión el

living in our glorious sunshine for a while, the lot of them finish up turning into native Spaniards.

LIEUTENANT CARDONA: That's exactly what's happening at the moment with the English in Gibraltar.

LIEUTENANT CAMPERO: And in Morocco. The only languages you hear spoken there are Arabic and Spanish.

LIEUTENANT CARDONA: Not even Tagalog?[1]

LIEUTENANT CAMPERO: An up-country Arab or two. Spanish is what most people speak.

LIEUTENANT CARDONA: I learned a bit of Tagalog in Jolo. I've forgotten it now. *Tambu*, that means "whore". *Nital budila*: "You dirty bastard". *Bedi tuki pan pan bata*: "I'm going to knock your bloody block off".

LIEUTENANT ROVIROSA: From the sound of it, your command of Tagalog is perfect!

LIEUTENANT CARDONA: Just enough for the basic necessities!

LIEUTENANT ROVIROSA: Exactly! I've forgotten even the little I knew, and I was in Mindanao for the whole campaign.

LIEUTENANT CARDONA: I spent five years in Jolo. The best years of my life!

LIEUTENANT ROVIROSA: Not everyone has had your luck. Postings abroad have been a nice racket for the top brass and for sergeants with desk jobs ... I've got nothing but bad memories of Midanao. I lost my wife and my right eye from a mosquito bite.

LIEUTENANT CARDONA: The isle of Jolo was paradise for me. Five years without a single headache, and I had my fill of eating, drinking and you-know-what whenever I fancied it.

LIEUTENANT CAMPERO: The fifteen-year-old native bints are very tasty!

LIEUTENANT CARDONA: Top hole! I used to give 'em a bath, stick 'em in a linen shirt and you'd think they were princesses.

His guffaws make the window-panes tremble, the ash from his cigar flies up around his chin, his belly swells out in Saturnalian glee. The coffee-cups dance on the table, the canary jumps around its cage and Lieutenant Lauro Rovirosa holds his glass eye in place.

LIEUTENANT CAMPERO: You dirty old dog!

LIEUTENANT CARDONA: It still gives me shivers of delight just to remember their little treasure-chests!

LIEUTENANT ROVIROSA: Gentlemen, allow me to remind you of the object of this meeting. A time-honoured duty requires us to safeguard the morals of our family, the family of the armed forces, as brave

---

1 A language spoken in the Philippines but not in Spanish Morocco!

heroico General Martínez Campos. Procedamos sin sentimentalismos, castiguemos el deshonor, exoneremos de la familia militar al compañero sin, sin, sin ...

EL TENIENTE CARDONA: Posturitas de gallina.

EL TENIENTE ROVIROSA: La frase no es muy parlamentaria.

EL TENIENTE CARDONA: ¿Queda o no queda admitida?

EL TENIENTE CAMPERO: Admitida. No nos ruborizamos.

EL TENIENTE ROVIROSA: Meditemos un instante y puesta la mano sobre la conciencia, dictemos un fallo justo. El apuntamiento reza así.

EL TENIENTE CARDONA: Prescindamos del cartapacio.

EL TENIENTE CAMPERO: ¡Conforme!

EL TENIENTE CARDONA: La cuestión está situada entre estos dos conceptos, que llamaremos de justicia y de gracia. Primero: ¿al teniente Don Pascual Astete y Bargas se le expulsa de las filas pronunciando sentencia un Tribunal de Honor? Segundo: ¿se le llama y amonesta y conmina, de un cierto modo confidencial, para que solicite la absoluta? Yo creo haber declarado que me pronuncio contra todos los sentimentalismos.

EL TENIENTE CAMPERO: ¿Qué retiro le queda?

EL TENIENTE ROVIROSA: ¡El máximo! No se muere de hambre. Todavía junta al retiro dos pensionadas.

EL TENIENTE CARDONA: ¡No hay como esos pipis para tener suerte! Este cura no tiene ni una pensionada. Y ha servido en Joló, en Cuba y en África.

EL TENIENTE ROVIROSA: Pero usted ha estado siempre en oficinas.

EL TENIENTE CARDONA: Porque tengo buena letra. ¡No me haga usted reír!

EL TENIENTE ROVIROSA: Usted poco ha salido a campaña.

EL TENIENTE CARDONA: ¿Es que solamente se ganan las cruces en campaña? ¡El Rey tiene todas las condecoraciones, y no ha estado nunca en campaña!

EL TENIENTE CAMPERO: ¡Ha estado en maniobras!

EL TENIENTE ROVIROSA: No es cuestión del Rey. El Rey es un símbolo, una representación de todas las glorias del Ejército.

EL TENIENTE CAMPERO: ¡Naturaca!

General Martínez Campos[1] once said. Let us not be swayed by any damn-fool sentimentality, rather let us punish this loss of honour and expel our brother officer from the bosom of the army without, without, without ...

LIEUTENANT CARDONA: Without fannying around.

LIEUTENANT ROVIROSA: Not an altogether diplomatic expression.

LIEUTENANT CARDONA: Do we record it or not?

LIEUTENANT CAMPERO: We do. We're no blushing schoolgirls.

LIEUTENANT ROVIROSA: Let us reflect for a moment and, with our hand on our conscience, pronounce a just verdict. The charge reads as follows ...

LIEUTENANT CARDONA: We can do without the small print.

LIEUTENANT CAMPERO: Hear! Hear!

LIEUTENANT CARDONA: The question lies between two principles, which we will term justice and mercy. On the one hand, do we, as a duly constituted Court Martial of Honour, pronounce sentence of expulsion from the ranks on Lieutenant Pascual Astete y Bargas? Or do we call him before us, confront him with his crime, reprimand him and order him, in a more or less confidential manner, to put in for an absolute discharge? I believe I have made my opposition to any wishy-washy nonsense absolutely clear.

LIEUTENANT CAMPERO: What sort of pension will he get?

LIEUTENANT ROVIROSA: The maximum! He's hardly going to starve. He's got two campaign pensions on top of the basic.

LIEUTENANT CARDONA: These squaddies have all the luck! This poor old soldier hasn't got even one campaign pension, and that's with active service in Jolo, Cuba and North Africa.

LIEUTENANT ROVIROSA: But you've always had a desk job.

LIEUTENANT CARDONA: Only because my handwriting is so neat. Don't make me laugh!

LIEUTENANT ROVIROSA: But you haven't seen much action.

LIEUTENANT CARDONA: Are you trying to tell me they only award campaign medals for active service? The King's[2] got all the medals going, and he's never been in action in his life!

LIEUTENANT CAMPERO: He's been on manoeuvres!

LIEUTENANT ROVIROSA: The King's got nothing to do with the case. The King's a symbol, an embodiment of all the glory of the Armed Forces.

LIEUTENANT CAMPERO: Absolutely!

---

1 Yet another right-wing figure in the officers' pantheon, Martínez Campos had led the *coup d'etat* of 1875 which re-established the Bourbon dynasty in Spain.

2 Alfonso XIII, who consistently used his role as titular head of the armed forces to meddle in military and political affairs.

EL TENIENTE ROVIROSA: Nos hemos salido de la cuestión, sin haber llegado a un acuerdo. Recapitulemos. ¿Se conmina privadamente al supradicho oficial para que solicite el retiro? ¿Le exoneramos públicamente, constituidos en Tribunal de Honor?

EL TENIENTE CARDONA: Propongo que se le llame, y cada uno de nosotros le atice un capón. ¿Es que vamos a tomar en serio los cuernos de Don Friolera?

EL TENIENTE ROVIROSA: Yo creo que sí. Oigamos, sin embargo, lo que opina el Teniente Campero.

EL TENIENTE CAMPERO: Es muy duro sentenciar sin apelación.

EL TENIENTE ROVIROSA: El fallo iría en consulta a la Superioridad.

EL TENIENTE CAMPERO: La justicia no excluye la clemencia.

EL TENIENTE ROVIROSA: ¡Evidente! ¿Quieren ustedes delegar en mí para que visite al Teniente Don Pascual Astete?

EL TENIENTE CARDONA: Por mí, delegado.

EL TENIENTE CAMPERO: Por mí, tal y tal.

EL TENIENTE ROVIROSA: Profundamente agradecido a la confianza depositada en mí, creo que procede reunirnos esta noche. Yo traeré un borrador del acta, y si ustedes están conformes, la firmaremos.

EL TENIENTE CAMPERO: Hay que pagar el café.

EL TENIENTE ROVIROSA: Yo soy huésped en la casa, y les convido a ustedes.

Los tres están en pie. Se abotonan, se ciñen las espadas, se ladean el ros mirándose de reojo en el espejo de la consola.

EL TENIENTE CARDONA: ¡Partamos a la Guerra de los Treinta Años!

LIEUTENANT ROVIROSA: We have allowed ourselves to be distracted from the main issue, without having reached agreement. Let me recapitulate. Do we privately coerce the above-mentioned officer into putting in for retirement? Or, as a duly convened Court Martial of Honour, do we publicly cashier him?

LIEUTENANT CARDONA: I propose we call him before us and each of us gives him a good clip round the ear. Are we really going to take Mr Punch the Cuckold seriously?

LIEUTENANT ROVIROSA: I believe we must. Nevertheless, let us hear Lieutenant Campero's opinion.

LIEUTENANT CAMPERO: To sentence him without right of appeal is rather harsh.

LIEUTENANT ROVIROSA: Our sentence is contingent on the approval of our superiors.

LIEUTENANT CAMPERO: Justice does not exclude mercy.

LIEUTENANT ROVIROSA: Of course not. Gentlemen, is it your wish that I should act as official delegate to go and see Lieutenant Pascual Astete?

LIEUTENANT CARDONA: I second the motion.

LIEUTENANT CAMPERO: Carried, *nem con.*

LIEUTENANT ROVIROSA: Profoundly grateful as I am for the trust vested in me, I deem it in order to convene a further meeting for this evening. I will bring a draft of the proceedings, and if you are both in agreement, we can all sign it.

LIEUTENANT CAMPERO: We haven't paid for the coffees yet.

LIEUTENANT ROVIROSA: I am a guest in this establishment, allow me to pay, gentlemen.

All three have risen to their feet. They button up their tunics, fasten on their swords and set their caps at a jaunty angle, looking at themselves out of the corner of their eyes in the mirror on the dresser.

LIEUTENANT CARDONA: Our country needs us![1]

---

1 The Thirty Years' War (1618-1648) demonstrated in reality a sharp decline in Spain's military power in Europe and even in the Peninsula, where she lost hegemony over Portugal. We convey the irony of Cardona's misplaced chauvinism by a reworking of a similar anachronistic call-to-arms from the Great War.

Escena novena

El huerto de Don Friolera, a la puesta del sol. La tapia rosada, los naranjos esmaltados de verdes profundos, el fruto de oro. La estrella de una alberca entre azulejos. Bajo la luz verdosa del emparrado, medita la sombra de Don Friolera: parches en las sienes, babuchas moras, bragas azules de un uniforme viejo, y jubón amarillo de franela. El Teniente aparece sentado en una banqueta de campamento, tiene a la niña cabalgada y la contempla con ojos vidriados y lánguidos de perro cansino. Manolita lleva el pelo sujeto por un arillo de coralina, las medias caídas y las cintas de las alpargatas sueltas. Tiene el aire triste, la tristeza absurda de esas muñecas emigradas en los desvanes.

MANOLITA: ¡Papitolín, procura distraerte! ¡A serrín! ¡A serrán! ... ¡Anda, papitolín!
DON FRIOLERA: ¡No puedo! Tu tierna edad te dicta esas palabras. Serás mujer y comprenderás lo que entre tu padre y tu madre ahora se pasa. Tu padre, el que te dio el ser, no tiene honra, monina. ¡La prenda más estimada, más que la hacienda, más que la vida! ... ¡Friolera!
MANOLITA: ¡Papitolín, no tengas malas ideas!
DON FRIOLERA: ¡Me quemo en su infierno!
MANOLITA: ¡Papitolín, alégrate!
DON FRIOLERA: ¡No puedo!
MANOLITA: ¡Ríete!
DON FRIOLERA: ¡No puedo!
MANOLITA: ¡Porque no quieres!
DON FRIOLERA: ¡Porque no tengo honor!
MANOLITA: ¿Papitolín, te traigo la guitarra para distraerte?
DON FRIOLERA: ¡Para llorar mis penas!

Manolita trae la guitarra. Don Friolera la saca de su funda de franela verde, y la templa con gesto lacrimatorio, que le estremece el bigote mal teñido. Los ojos de perro, vidriados y mortecinos, se alelan mirando a la niña.

DON FRIOLERA: ¡Eres la clavellina de mi existencia!
MANOLITA: ¡Papitolín, cuánto te quiero!
DON FRIOLERA: ¡Friolera!

Manolita, repentinamente compungida, besa la mejilla del viejo, que le acaricia la cabeza, y suspira arrugando el pergamino del rostro con una mueca desconsolada.

Scene Nine

Mr Punch's garden at sunset. The wall now pink; the orange trees enamelled with deep-green hues, their fruit golden. The star of a pond amid glazed tiles. Beneath the greenish light of a vine-arbour muses the shadow of Mr Punch; poultices on his temples, Moorish slippers, blue breeches of an old uniform and yellow flannel jerkin. The Lieutenant is seated on a camping stool. His daughter is sat astride him and he gazes on her with the glassy languid eyes of a lazy dog. Manolita has her hair tied back with a coralline ring, her socks round her ankles and the laces of her espadrilles undone. There is an aura of sadness about her: the absurd sadness that surrounds those dolls who have been exiled to the loft.

MANOLITA: Little daddy dumkins, try to raise a smile! To my derry, derry down! ... Smile please, daddy mine!

MR PUNCH: How can I? It's your tender years that make you utter those words. One day you'll be a woman and you'll realise what's going on between your mother and father now. Your father, my little treasure, he who gave you the gift of life itself, has been stripped of all honour. The most prized jewel of all – more prized than riches or even life! ... Oh deary, deary me!

MANOLITA: Daddy dumkins, don't think such bad thoughts!

MR PUNCH: I burn in their infernal flames!

MANOLITA: Please cheer up, daddy dumkins!

MR PUNCH: I can't!

MANOLITA: Smile!

MR PUNCH: I can't!

MANOLITA: It's only because you don't want to!

MR PUNCH: It's because my honour's been taken from me!

MANOLITA: Daddy, shall I bring you your guitar to cheer you up?

MR PUNCH: To sing the blues, more like!

Manolita brings his guitar. Mr Punch removes it from its green flannel cover and tunes it with a tearful gesture, which makes his badly dyed moustache tremble. His doggish, weak and glassy eyes gawp as he looks at the girl.

MR PUNCH: You're the pretty little flower of my life!

MANOLITA: Oh daddy dear, I love you so much!

MR PUNCH: Oh deary, deary me!

Manolita, with a sudden stab of pity, kisses the old man's cheek. He strokes her hair and as he sighs the parchment of his face wrinkles up in a disconsolate grimace.

DON FRIOLERA: ¡Lástima que seas tan niña!

MANOLITA: ¡Ya seré grande!

DON FRIOLERA: Yo no lo veré.

MANOLITA: ¡Sí tal!

DON FRIOLERA: ¿Tú no sabes que me he muerto esta noche? ¡Esta noche me han cantado el gorigori!

MANOLITA: ¡Te vas a volver loco, papitolín!

DON FRIOLERA: ¡Ya lo estoy!

MANOLITA: Con la guitarra te distraes.

DON FRIOLERA: ¡Se acabó el mundo para este viejo!

MANOLITA: Toca "El Contrabandista".

DON FRIOLERA: Veré si puedo.

Don Friolera recorre la guitarra con una falseta, y rasguea el acompañamiento de una copla, que canta con voz quebrada y jiponcios de mucho estilo.

COPLA DE DON FRIOLERA: ¡Ya se acabó mi ventura!
                          ¡Ya se acabó mi consuelo!
                          ¡Ya no tengo quien me diga
                          mi niño, por ti me muero!

En una buharda, por encima de los tejados, aparece la cabeza pelona de Doña Tadea Calderón.

DOÑA TADEA: Después del tiberio nocturno, ahora esta juerga. Tiene usted a todo el vecindario escandalizado, Señor Teniente!

DON FRIOLERA: ¿Qué pide el honrado y cabrón vecindario, Doña Tadea?

DOÑA TADEA: Para poner tachas, no es usted el más competente, Don Vihuela.

MANOLITA: ¡Cotillona!

DOÑA TADEA: ¡Mocosa! Con los ejemplos que recibes no puedes tener otra crianza.

DON FRIOLERA: A usted la cazo yo de un tiro, como a un gorrión. ¡Friolera!

DOÑA TADEA: Yo saco la cara por mi pueblo. Adulterios y licencias, acá solamente ocurren entre familias de ciertos sujetos que vienen rodando la vida ... ¡Falta de principios! Mengues y dengues y perendengues.

Fresca y pomposa, con peinador de muchos lazos, la escoba en la mano y un clavel en el rodete, asoma en el huerto la Señora Tenienta.

DOÑA LORETA: ¿Que picotea usted, Doña Tadea?

DOÑA TADEA: Primero son las buenas tardes, Señora Tenienta.

MR PUNCH: It's a pity you're still such a child!

MANOLITA: I'll be grown up one day!

MR PUNCH: I won't be around to see it.

MANOLITA: Of course you will!

MR PUNCH: Don't you know I met my death last night? Last night the banshee howled for me!

MANOLITA: You're going to drive yourself mad, daddy!

MR PUNCH: I already am mad!

MANOLITA: Play the guitar, it'll cheer you up.

MR PUNCH: It's the end of the line for this old soldier!

MANOLITA: Play "The Bootlegger with the Broken Heart".

MR. PUNCH: I'll have a go.

Mr Punch plays a trill on the guitar and strums the accompaniment to a ballad, which he sings in a quavering voice and with stylish flourishes.

MR PUNCH'S BALLAD: All my luck has now run out!
My comfort's finished, too!
There's no-one left to say to me,
"Sweetheart, I long for you!"

From a garret above the tiled roofs appears the hairless head of Doña Tadea Calderón.

DOÑA TADEA: After all the rowing last night, there's this racket now! You've got the whole neighbourhood scandalised, Lieutenant!

MR PUNCH: And what exactly does this most honourable toss-pot of a neighbourhood require of me, Doña Tadea?

DOÑA TADEA: You, my young minstrel boy, are in no position to throw stones.

MANOLITA: Slimy old muck-raker!

DOÑA TADEA: You snotty little brat! I'm not surprised about how you've turned out, though, given the example you've been set.

MR PUNCH: I'd bag you with my first shot, like I was out potting sparrows. Deary, deary me!

DOÑA TADEA: I'm sticking up for the whole town. Adultery and debauchery is what you expect from caravan-dwellers and their families ... Folk without principles! Slugs and snails and puppy-dogs' tails!

Unabashed and haughty, in a robe of many ribbons, a broom in her hand and a carnation in her hair-bun, the Lieutenant's Lady appears in the garden.

LORETTA: What are you wittering on about, Doña Tadea?

DOÑA TADEA: People usually say "Good afternoon" first, Loretta.

DOÑA LORETA: Para usted serán buenas.

DOÑA TADEA: Y para usted, pues tiene el bien de la salud.

DOÑA LORETA: Para mí son muy negras.

DOÑA TADEA: ¡La compadezco!

MANOLITA: ¡Cotillona!

DOÑA TADEA: ¡Dele usted un revés a esa moña! ¡Edúquela usted, Señora
          Tenienta!

DOÑA LORETA: Disimule usted, Doña Tadea.

DON FRIOLERA: ¡Niños y locos pregonan verdades!

DOÑA TADEA: ¡Chiflado! ¿Es conducta a la noche querer matar a la mujer, y
          ahora esta juerga?

DON FRIOLERA: ¿Halla usted la guitarra desafinada? Voy a templarla, para
          cantarle a usted una petenera.

DOÑA TADEA: ¡Insolente!

DON FRIOLERA: Ya me saltó la prima.

DOÑA LORETA: Mira si puedes empalmarla, Pascual.

DON FRIOLERA: Voy a verlo. No tiene muy buen avío.

DOÑA LORETA: ¡Son dos reales!

DON FRIOLERA: Ya lo sé, Loreta.

DOÑA TADEA: ¡Al cabo, son ustedes gente que viene rodando!

*Doña Tadea cierra de golpe el ventano, la Tenienta éntrase a la casa con un
remangue, y el Teniente rasguea la guitarra con repique de los dedos en la
madera.*

COPLA DE DON FRIOLERA: Una bruja al acostarse
                     se dio sebo a los bigotes,
                     y apareció a la mañana
                     comida de los ratones.

*Doña Tadea abre repentinamente el ventano, al final de la copla, y aparece con
un guitarrillo, el perfil aguzado, los ojos encendidos y redondos, de pajarraco.
Rasguea y canta con voz de clueca.*

COPLA DE DOÑA TADEA: ¡Cuatro cuernos del toro!
                   ¡Cuatro del ciervo!
                   ¡Cuatro de mi vecino!
                   ¡Son doce cuernos!

LORETTA: It might be good for you.

DOÑA TADEA: It's good for you as well. You've got your health and strength.

LORETTA: It's pretty awful for me.

DOÑA TADEA: I do feel sorry for you!

MANOLITA: Slimy old muck-raker!

DOÑA TADEA: Give that little hussy a good clip round the ear, Loretta! Bring her up decent!

LORETTA: Don't take any notice of her, Doña Tadea.

MR PUNCH: They say truth flows from the mouths of children and madmen.

DOÑA TADEA: You barm-pot! What sort of behaviour do you call this, trying to kill your wife last night and kicking up all this racket now?

MR PUNCH: Perhaps you find my guitar out of tune? I'll put it right and sing you a calypso.[1]

DOÑA TADEA: You cheeky ha'p'orth!

MR PUNCH: My top string's just broken!

LORETTA: See if you can fix it.

MR PUNCH: I'll see, but it's not very good quality.

LORETTA: It cost a tanner and all!

MR PUNCH: I know, I know.

DOÑA TADEA: When all's said and done, you're just like caravan-dwellers after all!

Doña Tadea slams the window shut. The Lieutenant's Lady lifts up her gown and goes into the house. The Lieutenant strums the guitar and flicks his fingers on the wood.

MR PUNCH'S CALYPSO: Once an old hag went to bed,
                    Smeared greasy make-up on her head.
                    When they found her the very next day,
                    The rats had eaten her all away.

Doña Tadea suddenly opens the window at the end of the calypso and appears with a ukulele. Her profile is jagged, her eyes beady and bright like a big bird's. She strums and sings in a decrepit old voice.

DOÑA TADEA'S CALYPSO: Four horns are on a bull
                     And on the stag another four!
                     With those upon my neighbour's head,
                     The score is twelve or more.

---

1 The *petenera* is a popular flamenco-style song. Although melodically different, it is not dissimilar to the calypso in terms of spontaneity and versatility.

Manolita corre por el huerto llenando el delantal de naranjas podres, y vuelve al lado de su padre. Don Friolera deja la guitarra sobre el banquillo, y pone en el ventano el blanco de un pim, pam, pum. Doña Tadea aparece y desaparece.

DOÑA TADEA: ¡Grosero!
DON FRIOLERA: ¡Pim!
DOÑA TADEA: ¡Papanatas!
DON FRIOLERA: ¡Pam!
DOÑA TADEA: ¡Buey!
DON FRIOLERA: ¡Pum!

Escena décima

La garita de los carabineros en la punta del muelle, siempre batida por la bocana de aire. Noche de luceros en el recuadro del ventanillo. Un fondo divino de oro y azul para los aspavientos de un fantoche. Don Friolera se pasea. Tras de su sombra, va y viene el perrillo. Don Friolera mece la cabeza con mucho compás. De pronto se detiene, y cruzando las manos a la espalda, hinca la mirada en el ángulo de sus botas, donde juega "Merlín".

DON FRIOLERA: ¡Vamos a ver! ¿No puedes estarte quieto un momento con la borla del rabo?

"Merlín" bosteza, y entre los colmillos alarga la lengua blanca, como si se consultase de sus males. Don Friolera le aparta con un signo estrambótico de sabio maniático. El perrillo se levanta en dos patas y hace una escala de ladridos en la segunda octava. Una gracia que le enseñó la Tenienta. Don Friolera siente el alma cubierta de recuerdos: el canario, la gata, la niña, la escoba de Doña Loreta. ¡El guitarreo desafinado de Pachequín! El perfil de bruja de Doña Tadea.

DON FRIOLERA: ¡Era feliz! ¡Friolera! ¡Indudablemente era feliz sin haberme enterado! ¡Friolera! ¡Friolera! ¡Friolera! El mundo es engaño y apariencia. Se enteran los mirones, y uno no se entera. ¡Ni de lo bueno ni de lo malo! ... ¡Uno nunca se entera! Yo me quejaba de mi suerte, y nada me faltaba. ¡Todo lo tenía dentro de mi jaula! ¿Cuándo me entero? ¡Cuando todo lo pierdo! ¡Cuando nada de aquello me resta! Estas trastadas no pueden ser obra de Dios. Al que las sufre, no puede pedírsele que colabore con el Papa. ¡Friolera! Este tinglado lo gobierna el Infierno. Dios no podría

Manolita runs through the garden filling her apron with rotten oranges, then returns to her father's side. Mr Punch leans his guitar against the bench and makes the window his target as a shy-at-the-Aunt-Sally stall. Doña Tadea bobs in and out of view.

DOÑA TADEA: Yobbo!
MR PUNCH: That's the way to do it!
DOÑA TADEA: Nincompoop!
MR PUNCH: That's the way to do it!
DOÑA TADEA: Silly ass!
MR PUNCH: That's the way to do it!

Scene Ten

The sentry post of the Customs Corps at the far end of the quay, battered, as ever, by gusts of wind. A starry night framed in the window: a divine backdrop of gold and blue for the gesticulations of a puppet. Mr Punch paces up and down. The little dog trots to and fro, chasing his shadow. Mr Punch shakes his head with a slow rhythm. Suddenly, he stops and, clasping his hands behind his back, fixes his gaze on the space between his boots, where Toby is playing.

MR PUNCH: Come on, now! Can't you stop that tail wagging for a moment?

Toby yawns and sticks his white tongue out as if he were being examined by a doctor. Mr Punch pushes him away with an exaggerated gesture that brings to mind a mad professor. The little dog stands up on its back legs and runs through a scale of barks in the second octave. It's a trick the Lieutenant's wife has taught him. Mr Punch's soul is inundated with memories: the canary, the cat, the little girl, Loretta's broom. Pachequín's tuneless guitar-playing! The witch-like silhouette of Doña Tadea.

MR PUNCH: I used to be happy! Deary me! There's no doubt about it, I was
          happy and didn't know it! Deary, deary me! This world is all
          deception and sham. It's the nosey-parkers that see everything,
          good or bad, and you don't see a thing yourself! ... You never
          realise! I used to complain about my lot, and I wanted for
          nothing. I had everything in my little nest! And when do I know
          it? Not until after I've lost the lot! When it's all gone! It can't be
          God behind these dirty tricks. You can't expect someone who's
          been caught by them to go along with what the Pope says. Deary
          me! This scene has been set up in Hell! God would never allow

consentir estos dolores. ¡Ni Dios, ni ninguna persona de conciencia! ¡Friolera! ¡Todo lo tenía y no tengo nada! ¿Qué iba ganando con dejarme corito el Padre Eterno? Le estoy dando vueltas, y este cisma no es obra de ninguna cabeza superior. Puede ser que Dios y Satanás se laven las manos. Toda esta tragedia la armó Doña Tadea Calderón. Con una palabra me echó al cuello la serpiente de los celos. ¡Maldita sea!

Entra una ráfaga de viento marino, y se arrebatan las hojas del calendario, colgado en un ángulo. La llama del quinqué se abre en dos cuernos. En la puerta, con la mano ante el ojo de cristal, está el Teniente Rovirosa.

EL TENIENTE ROVIROSA: ¡Buenas noches, Pascual!
DON FRIOLERA: ¡Buenas!
EL TENIENTE ROVIROSA: ¿Muerde ese perrillo?
DON FRIOLERA: No tiene esa costumbre.
EL TENIENTE ROVIROSA: Sin embargo, podría usted llamarle.
DON FRIOLERA: No hay inconveniente. ¡Ven acá, Merlín!

Don Friolera da palmadas en una silla. "Merlín" se encarama de un salto y, moviendo la borla del rabo, se acomoda.

EL TENIENTE ROVIROSA: Me trae un enojoso asunto.
DON FRIOLERA: Lo adivino.
EL TENIENTE ROVIROSA: Mi visita tiene un carácter a la vez privado y oficial. Un hombre de ciencia le llamaría anfibio. Yo no lo soy, y tampoco me creo autorizado para emplear esos términos.
DON FRIOLERA: ¿Quiere usted sentarse? Deja esa silla, Merlín.
EL TENIENTE ROVIROSA: Estoy más tranquilo con que la ocupe el perrito.
DON FRIOLERA: ¡Bueno!
EL TENIENTE ROVIROSA: Teniente Astete, un Tribunal compuesto de oficiales me comisiona para conocer los antecedentes del enojoso contratiempo ocurrido entre usted y su señora.
DON FRIOLERA: He resuelto no hablar de ese asunto.
EL TENIENTE ROVIROSA: No puede usted contestar en esa forma a mi requerimiento.
DON FRIOLERA: Pues así contesto.
EL TENIENTE ROVIROSA: Pascual, sea usted razonable.
DON FRIOLERA: No quiero.
EL TENIENTE ROVIROSA: Se expone usted a que los oficiales adoptemos una resolución muy seria.

such suffering. Not God, nor anyone with a conscience! Deary me! Once I had everything, and now I have nothing! What would God Eternal have to gain from stripping me bare? The more I think about it, the surer I am there's no higher intelligence behind this trouble and strife. Perhaps God and Satan have washed their hands of it. This whole tragedy was set up by Doña Tadea Calderón. With just one word she cast the serpent of jealousy around my neck! May she rot in Hell!

A gust of sea-wind enters, fluttering the leaves of a calendar hanging in the corner. The flame of the oil-lamp is blown into the shape of two horns. In the doorway, one hand covering his glass eye, stands Lieutenant Rovirosa.

LIEUTENANT ROVIROSA: Good evening, Pascual.
MR PUNCH: 'Evening.
LIEUTENANT ROVIROSA: Does that dog bite?
MR PUNCH: Not usually.
LIEUTENANT ROVIROSA: Still, I'd rather you called him over to you.
MR PUNCH: No problem. Here, Toby!

Mr Punch taps a chair with his hand. Toby jumps up on it and settles down, wagging the tip of his tail.

LIEUTENANT ROVIROSA: An unpleasant duty has brought me here.
MR PUNCH: I guessed as much.
LIEUTENANT ROVIROSA: The motive of my visit is both personal and official. I might call it amphibious, if I were a man of science. But I'm not, and I am therefore not authorised to use such terminology.
MR PUNCH: Would you like to sit down? Toby, off that chair.
LIEUTENANT ROVIROSA: I would feel more comfortable if the dog stayed on it.
MR PUNCH: Fair enough!
LIEUTENANT ROVIROSA: Lieutenant Astete, a Court Martial constituted by your brother officers has commissioned me to enquire into the circumstances of the disagreeable situation which has arisen between you and your good lady wife.
MR PUNCH: I have resolved never to speak of that matter.
LIEUTENANT ROVIROSA: That's no way to answer my demand.
MR PUNCH: That's all the answer you'll get.
LIEUTENANT ROVIROSA: Pascual, be reasonable.
MR PUNCH: I won't!
LIEUTENANT ROVIROSA: In that case, we might be forced to adopt very serious measures.

DON FRIOLERA: Pueden ustedes cantarme el gorigori.

EL TENIENTE ROVIROSA: No adelantemos los sucesos. En la reunión de oficiales se ha acordado que usted solicite el retiro.

DON FRIOLERA: ¿Y por qué? ¿Porque no tengo honor?

EL TENIENTE ROVIROSA: Sobre nuestras decisiones no puedo admitir controversia.

DON FRIOLERA: Mis cuernos no son una excepción en la milicia.

EL TENIENTE ROVIROSA: Respete usted el honor privado de nuestra gloriosa oficialidad.

DON FRIOLERA: Ningún militar está libre de que su señora le engañe. ¡Friolera! En ese respecto, el fuero no hace diferencia de la gente civil, y al más pintado le sale rana la señora.

EL TENIENTE ROVIROSA: ¡Evidente! ¡Pero se impone no tolerarlo! Los militares nos debemos a la galería.

DON FRIOLERA: ¿Y sabe usted mi intención oculta? ¡Pim! ¡Pam! ¡Pum!

EL TENIENTE ROVIROSA: No sea usted guillado y solicite el retiro.

DON FRIOLERA: ¿Usted qué haría en mis circunstancias?

EL TENIENTE ROVIROSA: Si contestase a esa pregunta, contraería una gran responsabilidad.

DON FRIOLERA: ¿Usted lavaría su honor?

EL TENIENTE ROVIROSA: ¡Evidente!

DON FRIOLERA: ¿Con sangre?

EL TENIENTE ROVIROSA: ¡Evidente!

DON FRIOLERA: Mañana recibirá usted en su casa dos cabezas ensangrentadas.

EL TENIENTE ROVIROSA: Real y verdaderamente se impone un acto de demencia.

DON FRIOLERA: ¡Y lo tendré!

EL TENIENTE ROVIROSA: ¡Chóquela usted, Pascual! Deploro que ese granuja no sea un caballero, porque me da el corazón que le hubiera usted pasado de parte a parte.

DON FRIOLERA: ¡Friolera!

EL TENIENTE ROVIROSA: Para mí, los desafíos representan un adelanto en las costumbres sociales. Otros opinan lo contrario, y los condenan como supervivencia del feudalismo. ¡Pero Alemania, pueblo de una superior cultura, sostiene en sus costumbres el duelo! ¡Para usted la desgracia ha sido la mala elección por parte de su señora!

DON FRIOLERA: La cegó ese pendejo.

EL TENIENTE ROVIROSA: ¡Evidente!

DON FRIOLERA: Mañana recibirá usted las dos cabezas.

MR PUNCH: You can dig a hole and bury me for all I care.

LIEUTENANT ROVIROSA: Let's not get ahead of events. The Tribunal of Officers has decided that you must put in for retirement.

MR PUNCH: What for? Because I've lost my honour?

LIEUTENANT ROVIROSA: I will not tolerate any questioning of our decisions.

MR PUNCH: What if I am a cuckold? There's nothing unusual about that in the Army.

LIEUTENANT ROVIROSA: How dare you insult the personal integrity of our glorious officer corps!

MR PUNCH: No soldier is exempt from his lady wife doing the dirty on him. Deary me! Where that's concerned, it's the same rule as in civvy street. Even the brightest spark can't stop the wife going crook on him.

LIEUTENANT ROVIROSA: Absolutely right! But they mustn't be allowed to get away with it! We officers have our reputation to live up to.

MR PUNCH: And you know what my secret intentions are? Bang! Bang! Bang! That's the way to do it!

LIEUTENANT ROVIROSA: Don't be such a fool, put in for retirement!

MR PUNCH: What would you do in my circumstances?

LIEUTENANT ROVIROSA: If I were to answer that question, I would be taking on a grave responsibility.

MR PUNCH: Would you cleanse the stain on your honour?

LIEUTENANT ROVIROSA: But of course!

MR PUNCH: With blood?

LIEUTENANT ROVIROSA: Certainly!

MR PUNCH; In the morning, two gory heads will be delivered to your door.

LIEUTENANT ROVIROSA: In all and absolute truth, a fit of insanity is exactly what's required.

MR PUNCH: And I shall have one!

LIEUTENANT ROVIROSA: Put it there, Pascual! I only regret that scoundrel is no gentleman, because I know in my heart you would have spitted him from gills to gizzard.

MR PUNCH: Yes, deary me!

LIEUTENANT ROVIROSA: In my view, duelling represents an advance in civilisation. There are some who think the opposite, and condemn it as a relic of feudalism. But Germany, that nation of superior culture, has retained the duel as a social institution. It was your bad luck that your wife made such a poor choice!

MR PUNCH: That creep pulled the wool over her eyes.

LIEUTENANT ROVIROSA: Of course he did.

MR PUNCH: The two heads will be delivered tomorrow.

EL TENIENTE ROVIROSA: ¡Deme usted un abrazo, Pascual! ¡Pulso firme! ¡Ánimo sereno! El Tribunal de Honor, fiado en la palabra de usted, suspenderá toda decisión.

DON FRIOLERA: Hágale usted presente mi gratitud.

EL TENIENTE ROVIROSA: Será usted complacido en tan honroso deseo.

DON FRIOLERA: Si hoy tengo perdida la estimación de mis queridos compañeros, espero que pronto me la devolverán.

EL TENIENTE ROVIROSA: Yo también lo espero.

DON FRIOLERA: ¡Pim! ¡Pam! ¡Pum!

"Merlín" endereza las orejas, y de un salto se arroja a la puerta de la garita, desatado en ladridos, terrible la borla del rabo. Don Friolera gesticula ajeno a los ladridos del faldero, y está, con una mano en el ojo de cristal y otra en el puño de la espada, el Teniente Don Lauro Rovirosa.

Escena undécima

Noche estrellada. Fragancia serena de un huerto de naranjos con el claro de luna sobre la tapia. Abre los brazos el pelele en la copa de la higuera. Cantan los grillos y se apagan las luces de algunas ventanas. El Barbero, encaramado a un árbol, apunta el tajamar de la nariz acechando una reja vecina, en las frondas de otro huerto. Doña Loreta, con peinador lleno de lazos, sale a la reja, y el galán saca la figura sobre la copa del árbol, negro y torcido como un espantapájaros.

DOÑA LORETA: ¡Pachequín!

PACHEQUIN: ¡Prenda adorada!

DOÑA LORETA: ¡Qué compromiso!

PACHEQUIN: ¿Te llegó mi mensaje?

DOÑA LORETA: ¡Estoy volada! A mí poco me importa morir, pero me sobrecoge pensar que peligra la vida de un sujeto de las circunstancias de usted, Pachequín.

PACHEQUIN: ¡Así habla el amor! Por lo demás, un hombre es como otro, y servidorcito no le teme al Teniente.

DOÑA LORETA: ¡Es un sanguinario!

PACHEQUIN: ¡Yo soy alicantino![1]

DOÑA LORETA: ¡Ay Pachequín, qué negra estrella! Si tomó una resolución de matarnos, la cumplirá, es muy temoso.

---

1 Literally, from Alicante. The translation attempts to preserve the humour of the malapropism.

LIEUTENANT ROVIROSA: Embrace me, Pascual! Keep a steady hand and a
     clear conscience! The Court Martial of Honour, accepting your
     word as an officer and a gentleman, suspends judgement.
MR PUNCH: Do me the honour of conveying my gratitude.
LIEUTENANT ROVIROSA: I will be delighted to carry out so honourable a
     mission.
MR PUNCH: If today I have fallen in the esteem of my dear comrades, I hope
     soon to rise again.
LIEUTENANT ROVIROSA: I hope so, too.
MR PUNCH: Take aim! Ready! Fire! That's the way to do it!

*Toby pricks up his ears and, with one jump, hurtles out of the door in a frenzy
of barking, the tassel on the end of his tail lashing furiously. Mr Punch waves
his arms about, oblivious to the pooch's howling, and Lieutenant Lauro
Rovirosa stands with one hand on his glass eye and the other on the hilt of his
sword.*

Scene Eleven

*A starry night. Serene fragrance of an orange-orchard with moonlight on the
white wall. The scarecrow-like figure opens his arms at the top of the fig-tree.
Crickets sing and the lights go out in some of the windows. The barber, high
up in a tree, aims the slicing edge of his nose, snooping at a neighbouring grille
in the leafy glade of another garden. Loretta, in her beribboned robe, appears at
the grille and her gallant raises his head above the top of the tree. He is black
and twisted like a scarecrow.*

LORETTA: Pachequín!
PACHEQUIN: My priceless jewel!
LORETTA: Oh dangerous liaison!
PACHEQUIN: Did you get my message?
LORETTA: I'm at the end of my tether! Death means little or nothing to me,
     but I go all a-tremble when I think that the life of such a fine
     figure of a man as your good self could be in danger.
PACHEQUIN: These are Love's own words! In any case, one man's pretty much
     the same as another and little old me is not afraid of the
     Lieutenant in the slightest.
LORETTA: He's as savage as a Berber!
PACHEQUIN: And I'm as crafty as a barber!
LORETTA: Oh Pachequín, what an evil star is this! If he's made up his mind to
     kill us, he'll go through with it. He's ever so pig-headed.

PACHEQUIN: Yo, donde le vea venir frente a mí, le madrugo.

DOÑA LORETA: Y se pierde usted, Pachequín.

PACHEQUIN: Nada me importa, si salvo la vida de una esposa mártir.

DOÑA LORETA: ¡Mi destino es morir degollada!

PACHEQUIN: ¡O de un tiro traidor! ...

DOÑA LORETA: Lleva una faca.

PACHEQUIN: Pues el sujeto que me avisó de andar con cautela le ha visto aceitar un pistolón.

DOÑA LORETA: Morir, no me importa.

PACHEQUIN: Ahora digo yo lo que me dijeron en cierta ocasión. La vida es muy rica.

DOÑA LORETA: Cuando hay felicidad, Pachequín.

PACHEQUIN: Tu felicidad es ser mi compañera.

DOÑA LORETA: No puedo abandonar mi obligación de esposa y madre.

PACHEQUIN: ¿Eso quiere decir que al considerarme correspondido me equivocaba?

DOÑA LORETA: Usted necesita una mujer sin compromisos.

PACHEQUIN: ¡Loretita, todo nos une!

DOÑA LORETA: ¡Mi honra nos separa!

PACHEQUIN: ¿Y la vida?

DOÑA LORETA: ¡Prefiero la honra a todo!

PACHEQUIN: ¡Mujer extraordinaria!

DOÑA LORETA: Como debo ser.

PACHEQUIN: Mi corazón enamorado no puede consentir que una esposa modelo sufra pena que no merece. Si ese hombre demente se satisface con beberse mi sangre, me avistaré con el. ¡Se la ofreceré en holocausto, a cambio de salvarte!

DOÑA LORETA: ¡Yo soy quien debe morir!

PACHEQUIN: Morir o matar, a mí me sale por nada.

DOÑA LORETA: ¿Y no vernos más? ¡Ay Pachequín, ésas no son palabras de un hombre que ama!

PACHEQUIN: Lo son de un hombre desesperado.

DOÑA LORETA: ¡No me sobresaltes! ¿Qué pretendes?

PACHEQUIN: Que mires de salvar tu vida.

DOÑA LORETA: ¡Dame tú el remedio!

PACHEQUIN: ¿Acaso no está manifiesto? ¡Pídele alas al amor! ¡Deja ese calabozo, deja esas tinieblas!

DOÑA LORETA: Calla. ¿Qué hombre eres tú? ¡Si me amas, calla! ¡No me ofusques! ¡Soy una débil mujer enamorada!

PACHEQUIN: ¡Muéstralo!

PACHEQUIN: Just let him try anything with me, I'll show him who's boss!

LORETTA: And what if you come off worst?

PACHEQUIN: It means nothing to me as long as I save the life of a wife and martyr.

LORETTA: It's my unhappy lot to have my throat cut from ear to ear!

PACHEQUIN: Or be the mark of a cowardly bullet!

LORETTA: But he's got a big knife.

PACHEQUIN: Well, the guy who warned me to watch my step has seen him oiling a blunderbuss.

LORETTA: Dying means nothing to me.

PACHEQUIN: I'd like to call to mind something that a certain person once said to me on some other occasion. Life is so sweet.

LORETTA: When there is happiness, Pachequín.

PACHEQUIN: Your happiness is to live by my side.

LORETTA: I cannot walk out on my duty as a wife and mother.

PACHEQUIN: Does that mean that in assuming that my sentiments were reciprocated I was mistaken?

LORETTA: You need a woman with no ties.

PACHEQUIN: Loretta dear, everything draws us to each other!

LORETTA: My honour keeps us apart!

PACHEQUIN: And our life together?

LORETTA: For me, honour comes above all else!

PACHEQUIN: You really are an extraordinary woman!

LORETTA: I do my duty, nothing more.

PACHEQUIN: My love-filled heart cannot consent that this model wife should suffer a punishment she does not deserve. If that madman can be satisfied by spilling every last drop of my blood, I'll do business with him. I'll offer up my life's blood as a sacrifice in exchange for saving you!

LORETTA: I am the one who must die!

PACHEQUIN: Dying or killing, it means nothing to me.

LORETTA: And never more to set eyes on each other? Pachequín, those are not the words of a man in love!

PACHEQUIN: They're the words of a desperate man.

LORETTA: Don't frighten me so! What is it you want?

PACHEQUIN: That you look to your safety.

LORETTA: Then tell me the remedy!

PACHEQUIN: Is it, perchance, not manifest? Pray to Love to give us wings! Leave this dungeon and its murky shades far behind!

LORETTA: Speak no more! What kind of man are you? If you love me, hold your peace! Don't bedazzle me so! I'm nothing more than a poor, weak woman in love!

PACHEQUIN: Then prove it!

DOÑA LORETA: ¿Y tú sabes a lo que te obligas? ¿Por ventura lo sabes? ¡Una mujer es una carga muy grande!

PACHEQUIN: ¡Una mujer, si media amor, es un peso muy dulce!

DOÑA LORETA: Luego sentirás el empalago.

PACHEQUIN: ¡Me calumnias!

DOÑA LORETA: ¡Tu desvío sería para mí una puñalada traidora!

PACHEQUIN: Juan Pacheco no da esas puñaladas.

DOÑA LORETA: ¿No tendrás ese descarte conmigo?

PACHEQUIN: ¡Pídeme el juramento que te satisfaga!

DOÑA LORETA: ¡Tirano! ¡Manifiesta claramente el sacrificio que pretendes de esta mujer ciega!

PACHEQUIN: ¡Que me sigas! ¡Te conduciré al fin del mundo! Lejos de aquí pasaremos por dos casados.

DOÑA LORETA: ¡Tentador, mira mis lágrimas, ya que mirar no sabes en mi corazón! ¡Juan Pacheco, soy madre, no pretendas que abandone al ser de mis entrañas!

PACHEQUIN: Concédeme siquiera venir una hora a mi casa. Cumple la promesa que me hiciste. ¡Loretita, has encendido el fuego de un volcán en mi existencia!

DOÑA LORETA: ¡Hombre fatal, no comprendes que si te sigo, me pierdo para siempre!

PACHEQUIN: ¡No te retendré!

DOÑA LORETA: Ni me harás tuya.

PACHEQUIN: Por la fuerza no apetezco yo cosa ninguna. ¡Recuerda mis procederes cuando te tuve en mis brazos! Baja al huerto, concédeme al menos hablarte con las manos entrelazadas.

DOÑA LORETA: ¡Ay Pachequín, tu conseguirás perderme!

PACHEQUIN: ¡Concédeme la gracia que te pido!

DOÑA LORETA: ¡Me pedirías la vida y no sabría negártela, hombre fatal!

La Tenienta se retira de la reja y sale al huerto. Se anuncia sobre la arena del sendero, con rumor de enaguas almidonadas. El galán, negro y zancudo, salta del árbol a la tapia lunera, y de la tapia al huerto. Cae, abriendo las aspas de los brazos.

PACHEQUIN: ¡Tormento!
DOÑA LORETA: ¡Tirano!

Doña Loreta suspira llevándose las manos a las sienes y el galán la abraza por el talle, bizcando un ojo sobre los perifollos del peinador, por guipar en la vasta amplitud de los senos.

LORETTA: Do you know what you're letting yourself in for? Have you the slightest idea? A woman is a very heavy burden!

PACHEQUIN: A woman, in Love's strong arms, is the sweetest load!

LORETTA: You'll soon grow weary of me.

PACHEQUIN: You do me an injustice!

LORETTA: If your ardour cooled, it would be a knife in the back for me!

PACHEQUIN: Johnny Pacheco doesn't knife people in the back.

LORETTA: So I wouldn't be just another woman to be left lying by the wayside?

PACHEQUIN: What assurance can I give that will satisfy you?

LORETTA: Tyrant! Say clearly what sacrifice you require of this poor bedazzled woman!

PACHEQUIN: Follow me to the ends of the earth! Away from here we can pass ourselves off as man and wife.

LORETTA: You wicked seducer, look at the tears I shed if you will not look into my heart! I'm a mother, Johnny Pacheco. Don't induce me to abandon the flesh of my own flesh!

PACHEQUIN: At least spend an hour at home with me. Keep the promise you made me, Loretta dear. You've kindled the fire of a volcano here in my breast!

LORETTA: You irresistible seducer! Do you not realise that if I follow you I should be lost forever?

PACHEQUIN: I will not hold you back!

LORETTA: Nor make me your own?

PACHEQUIN: No pleasure will I take through use of force. Be mindful of my correct deportment when I had you in my arms! Come down into the garden. Let us at least converse with our hands entwined.

LORETTA: Oh, Pachequín, you'll be the ruination of me!

PACHEQUIN: Merely grant me the favour I request!

LORETTA: You could ask me for my life itself and I'd know not how to refuse it you, you thief of my heart!

The Lieutenant's Lady withdraws from the grille and comes down into the garden. Her arrival is announced by the murmur of starched petticoats on the sand of the path. Her gallant, dark and leggy, jumps from the tree onto the moonlit wall and from the wall into the garden. He descends waving the sails of his arms.

PACHEQUIN: Torment of my every hour!
LORETTA: Tyrant of my soul!

Loretta heaves a sigh and raises her hands to her temples. Her gallant puts his hands round her waist and with one eye peers over the laces of her robe for an eyeful of the ample expanse of her breasts.

DOÑA LORETA: ¡La cabeza se me vuela!

PACHEQUIN: ¡Mujer adorada!

DOÑA LORETA: ¡Casi no te veo!

PACHEQUIN: ¡Arrebato de sangre, confusión de nervios, Loretita!

DOÑA LORETA: ¡Tendré que sangrarme!

PACHEQUIN: ¡Vida mía, me entra un escalofrío de pensar que te pinchen la vena!

DOÑA LORETA: ¡Zaragatero!

PACHEQUIN: ¡Negrona!

DOÑA LORETA: ¡Me pierdes!

PACHEQUIN: ¡Fea!

DOÑA LORETA: ¡Déjeme usted, Pachequín!

PACHEQUIN: ¡No puedo!

DOÑA LORETA: ¡Pero usted está siempre dispuesto!

PACHEQUIN: ¡Naturalmente!

DOÑA LORETA: ¡Qué hombre!

PACHEQUIN: ¡El propio para tus fuegos!

DOÑA LORETA: ¡Se engaña usted, Pachequín! Yo soy una mujer apática. Déjeme usted seguir mi suerte. Somos en el querer muy opuestos.

PACHEQUIN: ¡Me enciendes en una llama!

DOÑA LORETA: ¡Calla! ... ¡Pasos en la casa y abrir y cerrar de puertas! ¡Estamos perdidos!

Espanto y aspavientos. Se desprende del abrazo amoroso y pone atención a los ventanales del huerto. Pachequín, de reojo, mide la tapia y tiende la oreja con el mismo gesto palpitante que Doña Loreta.

PACHEQUIN: Me parece que ha sido un sobresalto inmotivado.

DOÑA LORETA: ¡Calla!

PACHEQUIN: ¡No oigo nada!

DOÑA LORETA: ¡La niña se ha despertado y llora de miedo! ¿No la oyes, tirano? ¿No te conmueve?

PACHEQUIN: ¡Vida mía, temí una tragedia! ¡Ya estaba con el revólver en la mano!

DOÑA LORETA: ¡Tú me perderás!

PACHEQUIN: ¡Si me amas, sígueme!

DOÑA LORETA: ¿No te conmueve el llanto de ese ángel?

PACHEQUIN: ¡Es fruto de tus entrañas, y no puedo menos de conmoverme!

DOÑA LORETA: ¿Y quieres que por seguirte desgarre mi corazón de madre?

LORETTA: My head is in a whirl!

PACHEQUIN: Of all women, most adored!

LORETTA: I can hardly see you!

PACHEQUIN: A sudden rush of blood, a tingling of the nerves, Loretta darling!

LORETTA: I'll have to have some blood let!

PACHEQUIN: My sweet, I go funny all over when I think of them putting the
        slightest prick in you!

LORETTA: Smooth-talker!

PACHEQUIN: Shady lady![1]

LORETTA: My ruination!

PACHEQUIN: Fit tart!

LORETTA: Let me be, Pachequín!

PACHEQUIN: That does not lie within my power!

LORETTA: But you're always ready for it!

PACHEQUIN: But of course!

LORETTA: What a man!

PACHEQUIN: The very man to burn in your flames!

LORETTA: You're mistaken, Pachequín! I'm an unfeeling woman. Leave me to
        my lot in life. We are the very opposite in love.

PACHEQUIN: I'm inflamed by just one spark from you!

LORETTA: Listen! ... Footsteps from inside the house and the door opening
        and closing! We're undone!

*Great fright and flailing of arms. She breaks free from the loving embrace and
fixes her attention on the windows overlooking the orchard. Pachequín, askance,
surveys the wall and cups his ear with the same quivering gesture as Loretta.*

PACHEQUIN: There's no need to get alarmed.

LORETTA: Sssh!

PACHEQUIN: I can't hear a thing!

LORETTA: My daughter's woken up and is crying because she's afraid! Can't
        you hear it, you beast? Has it no effect on you?

PACHEQUIN: Love of my life, I was fearful of some tragic occurrence! The
        revolver was already in my hand!

LORETTA: You'll be the cause of my perdition!

PACHEQUIN: If you love me, then follow me!

LORETTA: Are you not moved by the tears of that sweet angel?

PACHEQUIN: She's the fruit of your womb, so how could I not be?

LORETTA: Would you have a mother's heart cleft in twain through following
        you?

---

1 Literally 'dog-rough', and by antonymical extension 'good-looker'. An excellent
  example of how Pachequín mixes red-light slang with the rhetoric of melodrama
  and garbled officialese.

PACHEQUIN: Loretita, no es caso de conflicto entre opuestos deberes. Este nudo gordiano lo corto yo con mi navaja barbera. Tú me sigues y ese ángel nos acompaña, Loreta. Ve por tu hija. ¡Tendrá en mí un padre, como si fuese huérfana!

DOÑA LORETA: ¿Hombre funesto, sabes a lo que te comprometes?

PACHEQUIN: ¡No me hables más! ¡Madre atormentada, ve a por tu hija!

DOÑA LORETA: ¡Seré tu sierva!

PACHEQUIN: ¡Corre!

DOÑA LORETA: ¡Vuelo!

Jamona, repolluda y gachona, con mucho bulle-bulle de las faldas, toda meneos, se aleja por el sendero morisco, blanco de luna y fragante de albahaca y claveles. Pachequín, finchado sobre la pata coja, negro y torcido, abre las aspas de los brazos, bajo el nocturno de luceros.

PACHEQUIN: ¡San Antonio, si no me has dado esposa como es debido, me das una digna compañera! ... Te lo agradezco igual, Divino Antonio, y solamente te pido en esta hora salud, y que no me falte trabajo. En adelante tendré que mantener dos bocas más. ¡Son obligaciones de casado! ¡Mírame como tal casado, Divino Antonio! ¡Me hago el cargo de una familia abandonada! ¡Preserva mi vida de malos sucesos, donde se cuentan los acaloramientos de un hombre bárbaro! ...

Claro morisco de luna, senderillo perfumado de verbena. Con la moña desnuda en los brazos, sofocada, surge la tarasca. Pachequín abre el compás desigual de las zancas y corre a su encuentro.

PACHEQUIN: Yo te descargo del dulce peso.

DOÑA LORETA: ¡Gracias!

Al cambio de brazos, la moña pone los gritos en la luna. El raptor, negro y torcido, escala la tapia. Encaramado, alarga una mano al serpentón de la tarasca. Don Friolera, dando traspiés, irrumpe en el huerto, los pantalones potrosos, el ros sobre una oreja, en la mano un pistolón.

DON FRIOLERA: ¡Vengaré mi honra! ¡Pelones! ¡Villa de cabrones! ¡Un militar no es un paisano! ¡Pim! ¡Pam! ¡Pum! ¡No me tiembla a mí el pulso! ¡Hecha justicia, me presento a mi Coronel!

PACHEQUIN: Loretta, there is no conflict here between opposing duties. I can slice through this Gordian knot with my cut-throat. Follow me and bring that sweet angel with you. Loretta, go and fetch your daughter! She'll have a father in me, as if she were an orphan!

LORETTA: Do you know what you're letting yourself in for, you ruinous man?

PACHEQUIN: Not another word about it! Tormented mother, go for thy daughter!

LORETTA: I'll be a slave to you!

PACHEQUIN: Hasten!

LORETTA: I'll fly!

Buxom, chunky and charming, with a great swish of her skirts and all a-bustle, she goes off down the Moorish garden-path, bathed in moonlight, with the fragrance of basil and carnations. Pachequín, puffed up on his gammy leg, dark and wizened, opens the sails of his arms under the nocturne of the stars.

PACHEQUIN: Saint Anthony, you may not have given me a wife following the usual channels, but you've certainly given me a worthy companion ... And I thank you for it just the same. Oh Blessed Anthony, the only thing I ask you now is good health and plenty of work. From now on I've got two more mouths to feed. I've the responsibilities of a married man. Consider me just as that, most Divine Anthony, a married man and nothing more! I'm taking a destitute family under my wing! Keep me from all evil – especially from the raging fury of a madman!

Moorish moonlight, a path scented with verbena. The floozie looms up with the naked doll held excitedly in her arms. Pachequín opens the unequal compass of his shanks and runs to meet her.

PACHEQUIN: I'll relieve you of this sweetest burden.

LORETTA: Thank you.

As she is handed over, the doll sets up a wail to high heaven. The kidnapper, dark and wizened, climbs the wall. Once up, he stretches out a hand to his oompah-like floozie. Mr Punch stumbles out into the garden in his saggy breeches and with his peaked cap over one ear, a blunderbuss in his hand.

MR PUNCH: I'll avenge my honour, you scabby lot, just see if I don't! Town full of shit-houses! I'm a soldier, I'm no bleeding civilian! Bang! Bang! Bang! That's the way to do it! Steady as a rock my hand is! Once justice has been done, I'll hand myself over to the Colonel!

Dispara el pistolón, y con un grito los fantoches luneros de la tapia se doblan sobre el otro huerto. Doña Loreta reaparece, los pelos de punta, los brazos levantados.

DOÑA LORETA: ¡Pantera!

Nuevamente se derrumba. Algunas estrellas se esconden asustadas. En su buharda, como una lechuza, acecha Doña Tadea. Y se aleja con una arenga embarullada el fantoche de Otelo.

DON FRIOLERA: ¡Vengué mi honra! ¡Pelones! ¡Villa de cabrones! ¡Un militar no es un paisano!

Escena última

Sala baja con rejas: esterillas de junco; una mampara verde; legajos sobre la mesa, y sobre el sillón, con funda, el retrato del Rey niño. El Coronel, Don Pancho Lamela, con las gafas de oro en la punta de la nariz, llora enternecido leyendo el folletín de "La Época". La Coronela, en corsé y falda bajera, escucha la lectura un poco más consolada. Se abre la mampara. Aparece el Teniente Don Friolera, resuena un grito y se cubre el escote con las manos Doña Pepita la Coronela.

EL CORONEL: ¡Insolente!
DOÑA PEPITA: ¡Cierre usted los ojos, Don Friolera!
EL CORONEL: ¡Cúbrete con el periódico, Pepita!
DON FRIOLERA: ¡Hay sangre en mis manos!
DOÑA PEPITA: ¡Cierre usted los ojos, so pelma!

El Coronel aparta el sillón, y sale al centro de la sala luciendo las zapatillas de terciopelo, bordadas por su señora. Abierto el compás de las piernas, y un dedo alzado, se encara con Don Friolera.

EL CORONEL: ¡Cuádrese usted!
DON FRIOLERA: ¡A la orden, mi Coronel!
EL CORONEL: ¿Quién es usted?

He fires the blunderbuss and with a scream the moonlit puppets on the wall jump over into the next garden. Loretta reappears, her hair on end and arms in the air.

LORETTA: Savage beast!

She falls down once again. Some stars hide away, frightened. In her garret Doña Tadea lies in wait like an owl. With a rambling harangue the puppet Othello moves off.

MR PUNCH: I've wiped my honour clean, you stupid prannocks! You town full of stinking shits! A soldier's no bloody civvy!

Last Scene

A downstairs room with window-grilles. Cane chairs; a green-coloured screen; bundles of documents on the table, and above the armchair, in a frame, a picture of the King as a child. Colonel Pancho Lamela, his gold-rimmed glasses on the end of his nose, weeps sentimentally as he reads out the romantic serial from "The Epoch".[1] The Colonel's Lady, in corsets and underskirt, listens to the reading with an air of being in rather less need of consolation. Lieutenant Mr Punch appears, a scream rings out and Pepita the Colonel's Lady covers her bosom with her hands.

THE COLONEL: What insolence!
PEPITA: Shut your eyes, Mr Punch!
THE COLONEL: Cover yourself up with the newspaper, Pepita!
MR PUNCH: My hands are drenched in blood!
PEPITA: Keep your eyes shut, you ignorant lout!

The Colonel pushes his chair to one side and moves to the centre of the room, showing off his velvet slippers with a pattern embroidered by his wife. He stands with his legs stiffly apart and, with one finger raised, admonishes Mr Punch.

THE COLONEL: Stand to attention!
MR PUNCH: At your orders, Colonel Sah!
THE COLONEL: Name and rank?

---

1   These serialised sentimental tales were enormously popular: the soap-operas of their day.

DON FRIOLERA: Teniente Astete, mi Coronel.

EL CORONEL: ¿Con destino en la Ciudadela?

DON FRIOLERA: Así es, mi Coronel.

EL CORONEL: ¿Ha sido usted llamado?

DON FRIOLERA: No, mi Coronel.

EL CORONEL: ¿Qué permiso tiene usted?

DON FRIOLERA: No tengo permiso, mi Coronel.

EL CORONEL: ¡Pues a su puesto!

DON FRIOLERA: Tengo, urgentemente, que hablar a vuecencia.

EL CORONEL: ¡Teniente Astete, vuelva usted a su puesto y solicite con arreglo a ordenanza! ¡Y espere usted un arresto!

DON FRIOLERA: ¡Envíeme vuecencia a prisiones, mi Coronel! ¡Vengo a entregarme! ¡Pim! ¡Pam! ¡Pum! ¡He vengado mi honra! ¡La sangre del adulterio ha corrido a raudales! ¡Friolera! ¡Visto el uniforme del Cuerpo de Carabineros!

EL CORONEL: ¡Que usted deshonra con el feo vicio de la borrachera!

DON FRIOLERA: ¡Gotean sangre mis manos!

EL CORONEL: ¡No la veo!

DOÑA PEPITA: ¡Es un hablar figurado, Pancho!

El Coronel dirige los ojos a la puerta de escape, donde se asoma la Coronela. Jugando a esconderse, enseña un hombro desnudo, y se encubre el resto del escote con "La Época".

EL CORONEL: ¡Retírate, Pepita!

DOÑA PEPITA: ¿A quién mató usted? ¡Dígalo usted de una vez, pelmazo!

DON FRIOLERA: ¡Maté a mi señora, por adúltera!

DOÑA PEPITA: ¡Qué horror! ¿No tenían ustedes hijos?

DON FRIOLERA: Una huérfana nos queda. Me la represento ahora abrazada al cadáver, y el corazón me duele. El padre, ya lo ve usted, camino de prisiones militares. La madre, mortal, con una bala en la sien.

DOÑA PEPITA: ¿Tú crees esa historia, Pancho?

EL CORONEL: Empiezo a creerla.

DOÑA PEPITA: ¿No ves la papalina que se gasta?

EL CORONEL: ¡Retírate, Pepita!

DOÑA PEPITA: ¡Espera!

EL CORONEL: ¡Pepita, te retiras o te recatas mejor con el periódico!

DOÑA PEPITA: Si se ve algo, que lo lleven a la plaza.

EL CORONEL: ¡Retírate!

DOÑA PEPITA: ¡Turco!

MR PUNCH: Lieutenant Astete, Colonel Sir.
THE COLONEL: Posted to the garrison?
MR PUNCH: Correct, Sir.
THE COLONEL: Have you been ordered to report?
MR PUNCH: No, Sir.
THE COLONEL: Have you been given leave?
MR PUNCH: I have not, Sir.
THE COLONEL: Then back to your post!
MR PUNCH: Permission to speak on an urgent matter, Sir.
THE COLONEL: Lieutenant Astete, return to your post and request permission
          in accordance with regulations. And prepare yourself to be put on
          a charge!
MR PUNCH: Put me in the guardhouse, Colonel, Your Excellency. I have
          come to give myself up! Bang! Bang! Bang! I have avenged my
          honour! The adulterous couple lie weltering in their gore! Deary
          me! I don't wear the uniform of the Customs Corps for nothing!
THE COLONEL: A uniform you besmirch with the foul vice of drunkenness!
MR PUNCH: My hands are dripping blood!
THE COLONEL: I can't see any!
PEPITA: It's a figure of speech, Pancho!

The Colonel turns his eyes toward the doorway, where his wife is peeping out.
Pretending to conceal herself, she reveals a bare shoulder and covers up the rest
with the copy of "The Epoch".

THE COLONEL: Go to your room, Pepita!
PEPITA: Who did you kill? Come on, out with it, you berk!
MR PUNCH: I have slain my adulterous wife!
PEPITA: How dreadful! Don't you have any children?
MR PUNCH: There is one surviving orphan. I can imagine her now, clasped to
          the bosom of a corpse, and my heart aches for her. The father you
          see here before you, on his way to the cells. The mother, stone-
          dead, with a bullet in her brain.
PEPITA: Do you believe this tale, Pancho?
THE COLONEL: I'm beginning to believe it.
PEPITA: Can't you see he's pissed as a fart?
THE COLONEL: Go to your room, Pepita!
PEPITA: Not just yet!
THE COLONEL: Pepita, either leave the room or hold that newspaper up more
          carefully.
PEPITA: If he's seen anything, clap him in irons!
THE COLONEL: Leave at once!
PEPITA: Jealous Turk!

DON FRIOLERA: ¡Desde Teniente a General en todos los grados debe morir la esposa que falta a sus deberes!

DOÑA PEPITA: ¡Papanatas!

Arroja el periódico al centro de la sala y desaparece con un remangue, batiendo la puerta. El Coronel tose, se cala las gafas y abre el compás de sus chinelas bordadas, alzando y bajando un dedo. Don Friolera, convertido en fantoche matasiete, rígido y cuadrado, la mano en la visera del ros, parece atender con la nariz.

EL CORONEL: ¿Qué barbaridad ha hecho usted?

DON FRIOLERA: ¡Lavé mi honor!

EL CORONEL: ¿No son absurdos del vino?

DON FRIOLERA: ¡No, mi Coronel!

EL CORONEL: ¿Está usted sin haberlo catado?

DON FRIOLERA: Bebí después, para olvidar ... Vengo a entregarme.

EL CORONEL: Teniente Astete, si su declaración es verdad, ha procedido usted como un caballero. Excuso decirle que está interesado en salvarle el honor del Cuerpo. ¡Fúmese usted ese habano!

La Coronela irrumpe en la sala, sofocada, con abanico y bata de lazos. Se derrumba en la mecedora. Enseña una liga.

DOÑA PEPITA: ¡Qué drama! ¡No mató a la mujer! ¡Mató a la hija!

DON FRIOLERA: ¡Maté a mi mujer! ¡Mi hija es un ángel!

DOÑA PEPITA: ¡Mató a su hija, Pancho!

EL CORONEL: ¿Ha oído usted, desgraciado?

DON FRIOLERA: ¡Sepúltate, alma, en los infiernos!

EL CORONEL: Pepita, que le sirvan un vaso de agua.

DON FRIOLERA: ¡Asesinos! ¡Cabrones! ¡Más cabrones que yo! ¡Maté a mi mujer! ¡Mate usted a la suya, mi Coronel! ¡Mátela usted, que también se la pega! ¡Pim! ¡Pam! ¡Pum!

DOÑA PEPITA: ¡Idiota!

EL CORONEL: ¡Teniente Astete, ha perdido usted la cabeza!

DOÑA PEPITA: ¡Pancho, imponle un correctivo!

EL CORONEL: ¡Pepita, la vida de un hijo es algo serio!

DOÑA PEPITA: ¡Qué crimen horrendo!

EL CORONEL: Teniente Astete, pase usted arrestado al Cuarto de Banderas.

DON FRIOLERA: ¡Me estoy muriendo! ¿Podría pasar al Hospital?

THE COLONEL: From Lieutenant up to General, whatever the rank, the wife
     · who fails in her duty deserves to die!
PEPITA: You great ninny!

*She hurls the newspaper into the middle of the room and storms out, banging
the door. The Colonel coughs, puts his glasses straight and places his
beslippered feet further apart, raising and lowering his finger. Mr Punch, the
caricature of a fierce soldier, stands rigidly to attention, his hand braced against
the peak of his cap, his nose stuck up as if he were listening with it.*

THE COLONEL: What dreadful thing have you done?
MR PUNCH: I have cleansed my honour!
THE COLONEL: Are you sure it's not the wine talking?
MR PUNCH: Not at all, Sir!
THE COLONEL: You haven't had a drink?
MR PUNCH: I had a drink afterwards, to forget ... I've come to give myself up.
THE COLONEL: Lieutenant Astete, if what you claim is true, you have acted
           like an officer and a gentleman. It goes without saying that you
           have kept the best interests of the Corps and its honour at heart.
           Damn good show, have a cigar!

*The Colonel's wife, wearing a dressing-gown fastened with ribbons, bursts
excitedly into the room. She flings herself into the rocking-chair, one of her
garters showing.*

PEPITA: What a performance! He didn't kill his wife! He killed his daughter!
MR PUNCH: Oh no I didn't! I killed my wife! My little baby is an angel!
PEPITA: Oh yes he did! He killed the baby, Pancho!
THE COLONEL: Did you hear that, you wretched man?
MR PUNCH: Oh fiends, snatch at my soul!
THE COLONEL: Pepita, get him a glass of water.
MR PUNCH: Murderers! Cuckolded shits! Bigger cuckolds than me! I killed my
           wife! You kill yours, Colonel Sir! Kill her, she's at it an' all!
           Bang! Bang! Bang! That's the way to do it!
PEPITA: You cretin!
THE COLONEL: Lieutenant Astete, are you out of your mind?
PEPITA: Pancho, make him apologise!
THE COLONEL: Pepita, killing a daughter is a serious matter!
PEPITA: What a horrific crime!
THE COLONEL: Lieutenant Astete, report under arrest to the Guardroom.
MR PUNCH: I'm dying! Permission to report sick, Sir!

EL CORONEL: ¡Puede usted hacerlo!

DON FRIOLERA: ¡A la orden, mi Coronel!

EL CORONEL: Indudablemente ha perdido la cabeza. Explícate tú, Pepita: ¿Quién te ha contado ese drama?

DOÑA PEPITA: ¡El asistente!

THE COLONEL: Permission granted.

MR PUNCH: Very good, Sir.

THE COLONEL: He's clearly out of his mind. Tell me now, Pepita, who was it that gave you the real story?

PEPITA: Your batman!

Epílogo

La plaza del mercado en una ciudad blanca, dando vista a la costa de África. Furias del sol, cabrilleos del mar, velas de ámbar, parejas de barcas pesqueras. El ciego pregona romances en la esquina de un colmado, y las rapadas cabezas de los presos asoman en las rejas de la cárcel, un caserón destartalado que había sido convento de franciscanos antes de Mendizábal. El perrillo del ciego alza la pata al arrimo de una valla decorada con desgarrados carteles, postrer recuerdo de las ferias, cuando vino a llevarse los cuartos la María Guerrero: **El Gran Galeoto; La Pasionaria; El Nudo Gordiano; La Desequilibrada.**

ROMANCE DEL CIEGO:

> En San Fernando del Cabo,
> perla marina de España,
> residía un oficial
> con dos cruces pensionadas,
> recompensa a sus servicios
> en guarnición y en campaña.
> Sin escuchar el consejo
> de amigos que le apreciaban,
> casó con una coqueta,
> piedra imán de su desgracia.
> Al cabo de poco tiempo
> - el pecado mal se guarda -
> un anónimo le advierte
> que su esposa le engañaba.
> Aquel oficial valiente,
> mirando en lenguas su fama,

Epilogue

The market-place in a white town, facing the coast of North Africa. Blazing sunlight, playful sea-waves, amber-coloured sails, pairs of fishing boats. A blind man announces his street-ballads at the corner of a tavern, and the shaved heads of the prisoners can be seen at the barred window of the gaol, a tumbledown old building that used to be a Franciscan monastery back in the days before Mendizábal.[1] The blind man's dog cocks his leg against a fence covered in torn posters, the last remaining souvenirs of the holidays, when the María Guerrero theatre company was here to make a bob or two: "The Great Go-Between" : "Passion-Flower" ; "The Gordian Knot" ; "An Unstable Woman".[2]

THE BLIND MAN'S BALLAD.[3]

> In lovely San Fernando town,
> the jewel of Spain's South-West,
> there served a gallant officer,
> two medals on his chest:
> in barrack-room and battlefield
> he always did his best.
> His friends all tried to warn him
> but he brushed their fears aside.
> His goose was cooked the day he took
> a floozie for his bride:
> it was not long ere she'd fixed up
> a lover on the side.
> But sins cannot stay long concealed
> and scandal sure will out;
> an unsigned letter said his wife
> was putting it about,
> and, to his shame, his once-good name
> was now called into doubt.
> The gallant soldier burned like some
> volcano in his rage;
> his eyes shot sparks to see his name

---

1 Prime Minister and powerful political figure in the first half of the nineteenth century. He closed many religious institutions in 1835.
2 The theatre company of María Guerrero was the most prestigious in Spain in the first quarter of this century and frequently staged melodramas by Echegaray, such as the first and last of the titles displayed. *La pasionaria* (1883) was the work of Leopoldo Cano.
3 Such ballads, traditionally recited by blind performers, persisted in Spain even into the Franco era.

rasga el papel con las uñas
como una fiera enjaulada,
y echando chispas los ojos,
vesubios de sangre humana,
en la cintura se esconde
un revólver de diez balas.
Esperando la ocasión,
a su esposa festejaba,
disimulando con ella
porque no se recelara.
Al cabo de pocos días
supo que se entrevistaba
en casa de una alcahueta
de solteras y casadas.
Allí dirige los pasos,
la puerta encuentra cerrada,
salta las tapias del huerto,
la vuelta dando a la casa,
y oye pronunciarse su nombre
entre risas y soflamas.
Sofocando un ronco grito,
propia pantera de Arabia,
en astillas, de los gonces,
hace saltar la ventana.
¡Sagrada Virgen María,
la voz tiembla en la garganta
al narrar el espantoso
desenlace de este drama!
Aquel oficial valiente
su revólver de diez balas
dispara ciego de ira
creyendo lavar la mancha
de su honor. ¡Ay, no sospecha
que la sangre derramaba
de su hija Manolita,
pues la madre se acompaña
de la niña, por hacer
salida disimulada,
y el cortejo la tenía
al resguardo de la capa!
Cuando el valiente oficial
reconoce su desgracia,
con los ayes de su pecho
estremece la Alpujarra.

writ large upon that page;
he ripped and clawed the letter like
a lion in a cage!
He stuck his pistol in his belt,
but softly did he tread,
and buttered up his wife just like
a husband newly-wed,
while waiting till the time was ripe
to fill her full of lead.
Not many days had passed before
he learned that she was in
a place run by a certain dame,
a trafficker in sin,
where women, wed or single, went
to meet their fancy men.
His feet unerring there him led;
in vain he called and knocked.
He climbed a wall and tried the back,
but every door was locked.
And then his name on sinful lips
he heard abused and mocked.
A hoarse cry welled up in his throat,
like a panther did he leap.
The shutters splintered at the hinge -
What minstrel's heart's so cheap
that could conclude this fearful tale
and yet forbear to weep!
That soldier brave, all blind with rage,
did make his pistol roar.
A dozen bullets he fired off,
his honour to restore,
and little guessed his darling child
lay weltering in her gore.
How could he know the mother sly,
to allay her husband's doubts,
had made use of the little girl
as a pretext to go out,
and in her lover's cloak had wrapped
Manola all about?
When he found out that he had slain
the little girl he loved,
the groans he uttered up were such
the very mountains moved.

A la mujer y al querido
los degüella con un hacha,
las cabezas ruedan juntas,
de los pelos las agarra,
y con ellas se presenta
al general de la plaza.
Tiene pena capital
el adulterio en España,
y el general Polavieja,
con arreglo a la Ordenanza,
el pecho le condecora
con una cruz pensionada.
En los campos de Melilla
hoy prosigue sus hazañas.
El solo mató cien moros
en una campal batalla.
Le proclaman nuevo Prim
las cabilas africanas,
y el que fue Don Friolera
en lenguas de la canalla,
oye su nombre sonar
en las lenguas de la Fama.
El Rey le elige ayudante,
la Reina le da una banda,
la Infanta Doña Isabel
un alfiler de corbata,
y dan a luz su retrato
las Revistas Ilustradas.

Upon the guilty lovers then
his righteous ire he proved.
With an axe he's hacked off both their heads,
they lolled about so lewd,
he's grasped his trophies by the hair,
that gallant soldier-blue.
He stands before his general
and holds them for review.
It is a capital offence,
adultery, in Spain,
and brave General Polavieja,[1]
as custom doth ordain,
has on his chest a medal pinned,
as if for a campaign.
Today in the Moroccan Wars
his prowess marches on.
Five score of Arabs he laid low
in battle, with his gun.
The Bedouin warriors call him now
the new Napoleon.
The man who for the wagging tongues
was but a cuckold tame;
the man they once called Mr Punch
now owns a glorious name,
that rings out clear on every lip
in honour of his fame.
He's guard-of-honour to the King,
he's fêted by the Queen,
the Princess Royal has given him
a tie-pin, bright and clean.
His picture has a full page spread
in the Sunday Magazines.

---

1 The anachronism here (the veteran general Polavieja died in 1914) is deliberate:
Friolera has been incorporated into an absurdly out-of-date culture.

EPILOGO

Tras una reja de la cárcel están asomados Don Manolito y Don Estrafalario.
Huelga decir que son huéspedes de la trena, por sospechosos de anarquistas, y
haber hecho mal de ojo a un burro en la Alpujarra.

DON ESTRAFALARIO: Este es el contagio, el vil contagio, que baja de la
  literatura al pueblo.
DON MANOLITO: De la mala literatura, Don Estrafalario.
DON ESTRAFALARIO: Toda la literatura es mala.
DON MANOLITO: No me opongo.
DON ESTRAFALARIO: ¡Aun no hemos salido de los Libros de Caballerías!
DON MANOLITO: ¿Cree usted que no ha servido de nada Don Quijote?
DON ESTRAFALARIO: Ni Don Quijote ni las guerras coloniales. ¿No le
  parece a usted ridícula esa literatura, jactanciosa como si hubiese
  pasado bajo los bigotes del Kaiser?
DON MANOLITO: Indudablemente, en la literatura aparecemos como unos
  bárbaros sanguinarios. Luego se nos trata, y se ve que somos unos
  borregos.
DON ESTRAFALARIO: ¡Qué lejos de este vil romancero aquel paso ingenuo
  que hemos visto en la raya de Portugal! ¡Qué lejos aquel sentido
  malicioso y popular! ¿Recuerda usted lo que entonces le dije?
DON MANOLITO: ¡Me dijo usted tantas cosas!
DON ESTRAFALARIO: ¡Sólo pueden regenerarnos los muñecos del Compadre
  Fidel!
DON MANOLITO: ¡Con decoraciones de Orbaneja! ¡Ya me acuerdo!
DON ESTRAFALARIO: Don Manolito, gástese usted una perra y compre el
  romance del ciego.
DON MANOLITO: ¿Para qué?
DON ESTRAFALARIO: ¡Infeliz, para quemarlo!

Behind the bars of the gaol Immanuel and Straphalarius can be seen. It goes without saying they are lodged at His Majesty's expense, suspected of being anarchists and of putting the evil eye on a donkey up in the Alpujarras.[1]

STRAPHALARIUS: Its a contagion, a vile contagion, that decent, ordinary folk catch from literature.

IMMANUEL: From bad literature, Straphalarius.

STRAPHALARIUS: All literature is bad.

IMMANUEL: That can't be gainsaid.

STRAPHALARIUS: We haven't progressed any further since the novels of chivalry.[2]

IMMANUEL: Would you say Don Quixote has not had the slightest effect?

STRAPHALARIUS: Neither Don Quixote nor the Colonial Wars.[3] Don't you find it ridiculous, this literature of ours, so boastful you'd think it came strutting out from under the Kaiser's moustache?

IMMANUEL: There's no doubt about it, our national literature presents us as a bunch of bloodthirsty barbarians. But anyone who gets to know us realises we're as meek as lambs.

STRAPHALARIUS: What a world of difference between this contemptible balladry and that unpretentious little show we saw at the Portuguese border! That down-to-earth, malicious bit of fun had a completely different meaning. Do you remember what I said to you on that occasion?

IMMANUEL: You said so many things!

STRAPHALARIUS: Old Fidel's puppet-show is the only thing that can redeem us!

IMMANUEL: With a set designed by that paint-splasher Orbaneja! I remember now.

STRAPHALARIUS: Immanuel, fork out a tanner and buy that blind man's ballad.

IMMANUEL: Whatever for?

STRAPHALARIUS: To burn it of course, you dickhead!

---

1 A picturesque area on the south side of the Sierra Nevada, traditionally associated with smuggling.

2 Novels of chivalry, a genre popular in Spain in the sixteenth and early seventeenth centuries, satirised by Cervantes in *Don Quixote*.

3 The unsuccessful attempts by Spain in the nineteenth century to hold on to her overseas colonies.

Other modern authors from

HISPANIC CLASSICS

Federico GARCIA LORCA (1898-1936)

GYPSY BALLADS *(Romancero Gitano)* translated by R. G. Havard *(Aberystwyth)*
   Lorca's famous Gypsy Ballads were composed in the 1920s, when he was simultaneously obsessed by surrealism, gypsy culture and his own homosexuality. The combination of startling imagery with allusiveness rather than clarity has intrigued readers ever since, and Dr Havard explains most of it as being simultaneously an expression of his sexual interests and of his frustrating need to keep them secret. The translations are broadly into a free verse that aims to preserve the directness and the rhythm rather than the form, and will succeed in making the force of the original poems appreciated by English readers.
168pp; cloth ISBN 0 85668 490 2; limp ISBN 0 85668 491 0 (1990)

TWO PLAYS OF MISALLIANCE - THE LOVE BETWEEN DON PERLIMPLIN *(Amor de Don Perlimplín)* - and THE PRODIGIOUS COBBLER'S-WIFE *(La Zapatera Prodigiosa)* edited by V. F. Dixon *(Trinity, Dublin)*
   Lorca's *Amor de Don Perlimplín* and his *La zapatera prodigiosa* are often described as early and minor works. Yet the former was first performed only three years before his death in 1933, paired with a revised version of the latter, which he subsequently revised yet again. The translator argues that they are at least as accomplished and perhaps more characteristic than his more familiar rural tragedies.
cloth ISBN 0 85668 401 5; limp ISBN 0 85668 402 3 (In preparation)

MARIANA PINEDA - A Popular Ballad in Three Engravings, translated by R. G. Havard *(Aberystwyth)*
   "Careful scholarship and textual sensitivity underscore the appeal of this quality bilingual edition of Lorca's first theatrical success. Robert G. Havard meets the demands of poetry and literalness with praiseworthy balance . . This is a prestigious contribution, for it makes Lorca's youthful play more accessible to the English reading public" *Choice.* *182pp; cloth ISBN 0 85668 333 7; limp ISBN 0 85668 234 5 (1987)*

YERMA - A Tragic Poem in Three Acts and Six Scenes translated by I. R. Macpherson, and J. Minett *(Durham)*, with introduction by J. E. Lyon *(Bristol)*
   Perhaps the most famous and powerful of Lorca's plays, this edition has received both wide praise for its scholarship and recognition in performance. "The easy-flowing translation, which captures the essence of Lorca's masterpiece ... enhanced by John Lyon's excellent introduction to Lorca's life and work and Minett's perceptive discussion of the play" *Choice*; "the translation ... is both faithful and actable" *Vida Hispánica.* *144pp; cloth ISBN 0 85668 337 X; limp ISBN 0 85668 338 8 (1987)*

Antonio BUERO VALLEJO (born Madrid 1916)

A DREAMER FOR THE PEOPLE *(Un Soñador para un Pueblo)* translated by Michael Thompson *(Durham)*
    The dreamer of the title is the often maligned Marquis of Esquilache, the reformist minister of Carlos III. In this history play, the first of a remarkable series, Buero sets off Esquilache's relations with the king, the aristocracy, his wife and his maidservant against a lively recreation of the build-up of the famous 1766 Capes and Hats Revolt in the streets of Madrid. Public history and private tragedy are brought together in a complex dramatic structure, bringing into clear focus the clash between forces of change and immobility that lay at the heart of both the 18th century and the Franquist period in Spain. *cloth ISBN 0 85668 553 4; limp 0 85668 554 2 (In preparation)*

THE SHOT *(La Detonación)* edited by David Johnston *(Strathclyde)*
    Since the première of his first play, *Historia de una escalera*, in 1949, which restored serious drama to the post-Civil War stage, Buero Vallejo has been universally considered Spain's foremost living dramatist. *The Shot* must be considered as one of his most notable plays. It is historically important because it was the first play he ever wrote to be performed in post-Franco Spain and, as such, now reveals much about the forces underlying the creation of the new Spain. But it is also a masterly piece of dramatic literature in its own right, a finely crafted historical tragedy whose deep moral substance and quality of expression remind us that in 1977 Buero Vallejo was still a writer at the height of his creative powers. It deals with the life and suicide of another major Spanish writer, the nineteenth century satirist Mariano José de Larra with whom Buero easily identified, and is the last of Buero's major plays to be translated into English. *256pp; cloth ISBN 0 85668 455 4; limp ISBN 0 85668 456 2 (1990)*

Ramón María del VALLE-INCLÁN (1866-1936)

LIGHTS OF BOHEMIA *(Luces de Bohemia)* edited by John Lyon *(Bristol)*
    Written in the early 1920s, *Lights of Bohemia* is set in the twilight phase of Madrid's bohemian artistic life against the turbulent social and political background of events between 1900 and 1920. The play's protagonist, the poet Max Estrella, confronts the dilemma between art and social commitment and the problem of salvaging some sort of authenticity and identity in a context which converts him into an anachronism. This is the first play in a series of 'esperpentos' or 'grotesques' in whiich Valle-Inclan tries to convey the tragi-grotesque contradictions of his contemporary surroundings by the use of similarly contrasting registers in his theatre.
cloth ISBN 0 85668 564 X, limp ISBN 0 85668 565 8 (In preparation)

Pere CALDERS (born Barcelona 1912)

THE VIRGIN OF THE RAILWAY and Other Stories. Translated from Catalan by
Amanda Bath. Foreword by Geoffrey Pridham*(Department of Mediterranean Studies,
Bristol University)*
A first opportunity for English readers to sample some of the best short stories by the
contemporary Catalan writer, Pere Calders. His award-winning fiction, the fruit of more
than fifty years of intense literary creativity, are well-represented in this selection:

THE VIRGIN OF THE RAILWAY - *La verge de les vies*
AN AMERICAN CURIO - *Una curiositat americana*
RUSSIAN ROULETTE - *Ruleta russa*
TOMORROW AT THREE IN THE MORNING - *Demà, a les tres de la matinada*
THE BEST FRIEND - *El millor amic*
THE GOLDEN AGE and THE EXPRESS - *L'edat d'or i L'exprés*
NATURAL HISTORY - *Història natural*
THE DOMESTIC TREE - *L'arbre domèstic*
HEDERA HELIX - *L' "Hedera Helix"*
THE SPIRAL - *L'espiral*

Calders' "magic-realist" vision, his playful depiction of man's struggles for survival in a
20th century urban environment, and his humorous tales of "science" and the
supernatural will appeal to young and old alike.
160pp; cloth ISBN 0 85668 546 1 limp ISBN 0 85668 547 X

*For further information and catalogues on oriental, classical and ancient history and
literature please write to*

ARIS & PHILLIPS LTD.,
Teddington House, Warminster, Wiltshire BA12 8PQ England